FTB

DATE DUE

Wi... y Lin

Th... t

D0106788

VOLO
an imprint of
HYPERION BOOKS FOR CHILDREN
New York

© 2004 Disney Enterprises, Inc.

W.I.T.C.H. Will Irma Taranee Cornelia Hay Lin is a trademark of Disney Enterprises, Inc.
Volo® is a registered trademark of Disney Enterprises, Inc.
Volo/Hyperion Books for Children are imprints of Disney Children's Group, L.L.C.

Printed in the United States of America
First Edition
1 3 5 7 9 10 8 6 4 2

This book is set in 12/16.5 Hiroshige Book.
ISBN 0-7868-5139-2
Visit www.clubwitch.com

MERIDIAN

HAVE YOU MADE UP YOUR MIND YET, YOUR HIGHNESS?

I . . . I'M NOT SURE. ALL YOUR GOWNS ARE SO BEAUTIFUL. . . .

A SPECIAL DAY CALLS FOR A SPECIAL GOWN. . . .

. . . AND YOUR CORONATION WILL DEFINITELY BE A SPECIAL AND UNFORGETTABLE DAY FOR THE ENTIRE CITY.

HMMM . . . WELL, I'LL THINK ABOUT THESE DRESSES FOR A LITTLE WHILE, MASTER JINK. THEN I'LL LET YOU KNOW WHICH ONE.

IF YOU WANT MY OPINION . . .

. . . I WOULD HAVE ASKED FOR IT. WHERE'S MY BROTHER?

PRINCE PHOBOS IS MEETING WITH HIS MURMURERS.

I SEE.

AH, LISTEN, CEDRIC . . .

. . . I'VE NOTICED THAT IN PUBLIC, YOU DON'T CALL ME BY NAME. YOU USE THE TITLE "YOUR HIGHNESS". . . .

A COURTESY WORTHY OF A PERSON OF YOUR RANK.

WELL, FROM NOW ON, I'D LIKE YOU TO SHOW ME THE SAME COURTESY IN **PRIVATE** AS WELL.

B—BUT . . . OF COURSE. AS YOU WISH, YOUR HIGHNESS.

THE NERVE OF THAT GIRL. A FEW WEEKS AGO SHE WOULDN'T HAVE DARED TO TREAT ME THIS WAY.

RECENT EVENTS MUST HAVE TRIGGERED SOMETHING IN THAT LITTLE HEAD OF HERS.

I'D BETTER INFORM THE PRINCE IMMEDIATELY. HE'LL WANT TO KNOW OF THIS DEVELOPMENT.

ENLIGHTENED COURT OF MURMURERS, VOICE AND EYES OF THE PRINCE OF PRINCES.

I ASK YOUR LEAVE TO CONSULT WITH OUR POWERFUL LORD.

I WAS EXPECTING YOU, CEDRIC. YOU ALWAYS ARRIVE AT JUST THE RIGHT MOMENT. . . .

. . . JOIN ME WITHOUT FEAR. . . . IN THE ABYSS OF SHADOWS!

. . . ABYSS OF SHAD—

. . . OF SHADOWS . . .

THE CITY IS FILLED WITH EXCITEMENT AND ANTICIPATION. BOTH THE REBEL GROUPS AND THE CITIZENS OF MERIDIAN EXPECT A GREAT DEAL FROM ELYON. . . .

YES, WILL! THE PRINCE IS A CRUEL, POWER-HUNGRY CREATURE. HE WOULD NEVER RELINQUISH THE THRONE TO HIS SISTER— NOT WITHOUT A FIGHT.

I CAN UNDERSTAND THAT. I EVEN FIGHT WITH MY BROTHER ABOUT WHO GETS TO SIT IN THE FRONT SEAT OF THE CAR. . . .

BUT YOU'RE WORRIED THAT PHOBOS IS PLOTTING SOMETHING, RIGHT?

SO WHY IS HE GOING THROUGH WITH THE CEREMONY, THEN?

I'VE BEEN ASKING MYSELF THE SAME QUESTION. ELYON NEEDS TO FIGURE IT OUT. . . . BUT I DON'T KNOW IF SHE WILL.

THAT POOR GIRL IS ALL ALONE, AND IS UNDER THE INFLUENCE OF PHOBOS AND CEDRIC. . . .

NOT AS MUCH AS YOU MAY THINK. ELYON HAS BEEN CHANGING RECENTLY. I KNOW IT.

MAYBE THAT'S EXACTLY WHAT'S MAKING THE PRINCE NERVOUS ENOUGH TO PUSH UP THE CEREMONY. ANNOUNCING THE CORONATION WAS A VERY SUDDEN DECISION.

BUT THEN . . . WHAT CAN WE DO?

I'D LIKE YOU TO KEEP AN EYE ON ELYON AND MAKE SURE THAT SHE DOESN'T GET HURT!

ONE

Sergeant Lair was worried. As he hurried down the quiet Heatherfield street early in the morning, his concern was not about his daughter, Irma: he was thinking about Irma's friend Elyon. Elyon Brown and her family had mysteriously disappeared, and Sergeant Lair wanted to get to the bottom of the mystery.

He continued to shake his head as he walked up to the deserted Brown home. He had dropped Irma off there many times for playdates with the sweet girl. Elyon was very quiet and loved to draw, he recalled as he put a key in the front door. He glanced around the living room of the two-story house in Heatherfield, a seaside city. Of all the crimes that he had investigated, this one was the most disturbing to him.

As he walked through the empty house, he couldn't help wondering what had happened. There was no sign of burglary or arson. No signs or clues at all had been left.

Yes, Sergeant Lair thought with a sigh, the average officer would find nothing remarkable in this room. There were no glaring clues or noticeably misplaced items. To the untrained eye, it looked as if nothing were wrong.

That, Sergeant Lair noted, is what I find *most* troubling. A whole family vanishes from this house and not a ripple is felt, inside or outside its walls. Nobody even reports the family's disappearance! It's as if these people just dropped into Heatherfield out of nowhere, then went right back to nowhere when they left.

As he scanned the living room, Sergeant Lair's eyes fell upon a snapshot in an antique, silver frame. The man and woman in the picture were slight and pale, but their large, wide eyes sparkled happily. Sitting between them was a petite young girl. She was leaning her head on her mother's shoulder, giggling.

They're all gone, Sergeant Lair thought. Eleanor and Thomas Brown and their daughter, Elyon. Elyon—who was a student at the

Sheffield Institute with Irma; who came to Irma's slumber party last spring; who was almost exactly my daughter's age.

The thought made Sergeant Lair's stomach lurch in fear. He might have been a hardened detective, but he was a big softie when it came to his family—especially Irma and little Christopher.

Maybe, he thought, I should start making her come straight home after school, with no stops at the mall or at her friends' houses.

As soon as he finished the thought, Sergeant Lair rolled his eyes. That'd go over like a flying turtle, he thought.

He could only imagine the weeping, wailing, and dramatic monologues Irma would employ to win back her freedom. Especially these days.

I barely see Irma anymore, Sergeant Lair realized with a frown. She spends every spare minute with her friends. It's always the same girls—Will, Hay Lin, Cornelia, and Taranee. And they're so secretive! When they came over for dinner the other night, there was so much whispering going on I could have sworn they were up to something.

Maybe Hay Lin has them all involved in an

art project, Sergeant Lair thought. She's such an imaginative girl, always scribbling things on her hands with Magic Markers and rigging up kooky outfits for herself. I don't think I've ever seen that little girl without a pair of goggles strapped to her head or a bungee cord looped around her waist.

Sergeant Lair opened the door beneath the stairs. It swung on its hinges with a tired *creeeak*.

Bang! Bangbangbang!

"Ugh! This is impossible!" a man grunted.

"Huh?" Sergeant Lair whispered. He peered down a precarious staircase into the basement. When his eyes had adjusted to the dim light, he saw a strange, circular room that looked as claustrophobic as a tomb. The walls were made of metal panels locked together with soldered seams. Banging on one of those panels with a hammer was a burly, blond man. His broad chest was heaving with the effort of swinging the hammer.

Sergeant Lair instantly recognized Agent Joel McTiennan, and the agent was *not* happy.

McTiennan and his petite partner, Agent Maria Medina, worked for Interpol. Sergeant

Lair had asked Interpol for its help in cracking the Brown case. Big Guy and Small Fry—as the odd couple were known to their colleagues— had arrived in Heatherfield with lots of fancy tools and techniques, but had yet to come up with many clues. The agents had come up with nothing after joining the Lairs for dinner a few nights earlier, when Irma and her friends had been over. The five girls had known Elyon, yet they'd been completely evasive on the subject of her disappearance.

That *was* sort of strange, Sergeant Lair grumbled to himself. Usually, Irma loves to talk people's ear off. It's her favorite thing to do, besides taking endless baths and watching *Boy Comet* on TV.

Poor Irma, Sergeant Lair concluded. She and her friends must be so upset about Elyon. I can't think of another time when Irma was so upset that she was speechless. Sighing sympathetically, the detective returned his attention to the agents.

"Step aside, Medina," McTiennan said to his partner. He had just reached into his toolbox for a bigger tool—a heavy, large sledgehammer.

Rolling up the sleeves of his blue shirt, McTiennan gripped the sledgehammer in both hands. He reared back and swung the hammer into the metal wall.

Clang! Went the hammerhead against the metal panel.

Tlak!

Oooh, Sergeant Lair thought with a cringe. Only one blow snapped that hammer's handle like a twig!

"Drat!" McTiennan shouted. He caught the hammerhead before it landed on his foot, then stared at the broken tool in frustration.

Medina sighed as she looked at her partner. "Let's make that your last try, McTiennan," she declared. "You can have another little 'chat' with the wall tomorrow morning."

"I could try using dynamite," McTiennan suggested as he tossed his broken hammer into his toolbox.

"If the Brown family does come back," Medina teased, "it would be nice if they found their house still here, don't you think?"

"*If* they come back, I'll ask them to explain what all of this is about," McTiennan spat.

This? Sergeant Lair thought, wondering

what the two agents had found. I think I need to know what these two are talking about.

He cleared his throat. McTiennan's blond, shaggy head and Medina's brunette one turned his way. Sergeant Lair waved from the top of the basement stairs. "Still nothing, detectives?" he asked politely.

"Unfortunately, nothing," Medina confirmed. "All that the echo-detector did was prove what we already know."

Medina pointed to the gadget, which was wired to the base of the wall. As Sergeant Lair walked down the stairs, he could see the needle in the detector's gauge jumping and trembling. When he reached Medina's side, she pulled a map out of her bag and unrolled it for him.

"The echo-detector tells us that there is an enormous area behind this wall," she said. "An area that doesn't appear on the house's blueprints."

"Sure looks like our missing family had something to hide," McTiennan said, giving the basement wall a surly glance.

"No doubt about it," his partner agreed. Behind Medina's businesslike spectacles, Sergeant Lair thought he detected a flash of worry. Her hand shook slightly as she pressed a palm against the wall.

"And the Browns," Medina added, "have done a really good job of disappearing."

TWO

Cornelia tromped down the sidewalk with Will, Irma, Taranee, and Hay Lin. Her head was still buzzing with the ominous news that Mrs. Rudolph had just delivered. It was strange that her friends had once been afraid of the very odd teacher who taught math at the Sheffield Institute. At first, Cornelia thought that Irma's dislike of math was the thing that made her not trust the quiet new teacher. After some investigation, though, it became clear that Mrs. Rudolph was simply not like other teachers at school. She was entirely from another universe! But now the girls knew that Mrs. Rudolph was an important link to the world of Metamoor—and to Elyon.

"I'd like you to keep an eye on Elyon and to

make sure that she doesn't get hurt," Mrs. Rudolph had said. Those words still echoed in Cornelia's head. She looked at her friends in a panic. Could they really protect Elyon from Phobos's evil plan?

Cornelia dug her hands deeper into the pockets of her gray shearling jacket. She shivered as a gust of late winter wind ruffled her long, blond hair.

Of course, she thought drily, Elyon's been in trouble for a long time—ever since she defected from Heatherfield and took up residence in the gloomy world of Metamoor.

Cornelia shook her head slowly. It seemed very long ago that her best friend had disappeared from Heatherfield. Cornelia missed her so much. Elyon had truly understood her feelings about Caleb, her dream boy from Metamoor.

This whole mess had started when Elyon had met a guy who she thought was cute. That was not so unusual: Elyon was always mooning over some boy from biology class, or crushing on her science-project partner. But this boy—a young man, really—had been different. He had shown up at the Sheffield Institute's

Halloween dance, looking supermysterious and very sophisticated.

If only we'd known just how mysterious he would turn out to be! Cornelia thought with a frown.

The boy had introduced himself to Elyon as Cedric. He'd asked Elyon out before they'd exchanged more than a dozen words! And unlike some average guy, he hadn't been interested in just an average movie date.

He'd wanted Elyon to meet him at the Sheffield gym.

Filled with nervous excitement, Will, Irma, and Hay Lin joined Elyon at the meeting place.

When the friends showed up at the gym, though, Elyon had been nowhere to be found. Unfortunately, a giant monster had been there instead. They hadn't known it at the time, but Cedric had morphed from a long-haired hottie into a giant serpent with ripped arms, a razor-sharp chin, and menacing, red eyes.

He was a creature from Metamoor.

Ah, Metamoor, Cornelia thought. And the city of Meridian: a dark and miserable place. At least, that's been the case under its current ruler, Prince Phobos.

Phobos shouldn't have been the ruler of Metamoor. No man was supposed to assume that role. The royal power had always been passed down from queen to queen.

The last queen, though, had died years ago. Her son had taken the throne, but the rightful heir had actually been the queen's daughter— Elyon.

Who would have guessed? Cornelia wondered: after being best friends with her forever, she never would have thought that Elyon's history was so different from her own. Elyon was a real princess! She had been born into Meridian's royal family, destined to rule Metamoor one day. Her parents' deaths had changed that plan, though. Elyon's greedy older brother, Prince Phobos, had seen a great opportunity in the tragedy of their parents' deaths. He had set out to absorb his sister's powers and use them to conquer the universe!

The whole plan would have gone off without a hitch if three rebel leaders hadn't kidnapped the baby Elyon and spirited her away to a safe place.

That safe place happened to be none other than Heatherfield. The three rebels had morphed into human shapes. Two of them had become Elyon's "parents," Thomas and Elyon Brown. The third rebel, Elyon's nanny, had become that Sheffield math teacher, Mrs. Rudolph.

And why wasn't Phobos able to chase after the trio and snatch Elyon back?

We have the Veil and the Oracle of Candracar to thank for that, Cornelia thought, glancing up high above her head. Lucky for us, Metamoor isn't the only alternate realm lurking out there. There's also Candracar, an ethereal temple in the heart of infinity. A mysterious place—home to wise beings who watch over the universe and constantly work to keep the balance between good and evil.

The most powerful of those beings was the Oracle. To protect the earth from evil, he and the Congregation had created the Veil: an invisible, but impenetrable, blockade between the worlds. Nothing bad could cross that supernatural barrier.

That is, Cornelia thought with a sigh, until the millennium hit.

The start of the millennium had unleashed powerful cosmic forces that had weakened the

Veil. Twelve holes had been torn open that became tunnels—portals—between Metamoor and the earth. And all of those portals were right there in Heatherfield.

Cornelia looked around at her hometown's innocuous brick buildings and lush trees, and at the fashionably dressed people hurrying to school and work.

You'd never know, Cornelia sighed, that portals to an alternate universe lurked all over this town—in Mrs. Rudolph's attic, in the Sheffield gym, in a shell-shaped cave on the beach, *and* in Elyon's basement. In fact, nobody knows about those passageways except the five of us—Will, Irma, Taranee, Hay Lin, and me. Together we make up a group that we like to call W.I.T.C.H—all of our initials combined!

More important than that, Cornelia thought, is the fact that we are infused with special powers!

Cornelia, for instance, had discovered that she had the power to manipulate the earth. She could make plants grow in an instant, blast holes in bricks, and make the ground tremble beneath her feet.

Hay Lin, meanwhile, was as carefree as air. With a flick of her finger, she'd whip up winds, conjure cyclones, and even lift herself into the air. She was the only one who could actually fly—and that fit her breezy personality.

Finally, Irma had power over water, and Taranee was in control of fire.

The only thing the girls couldn't do was figure out why they'd developed their perplexing powers.

Then one afternoon at Hay Lin's apartment, they'd found out. While the girls had been discussing how strange their lives had become, Hay Lin's grandmother had glided into the room. Cornelia had always loved Hay Lin's grandmother. Not only was she always generous with her homemade almond cookies and her amusing fables but she'd also carried herself with a wonderful air of mystery.

That afternoon, Cornelia had discovered the reason behind the old woman's secretive manner. Hay Lin's grandmother was not just some sweet, silver-haired old lady. She was also a former Guardian of the Veil! When she had been a young girl, the Oracle of Candracar had anointed her as such, to protect the Veil, should it ever be breached by enemies.

Now that the Veil was full of holes, Hay Lin's grandmother was passing the torch.

After telling Cornelia, Irma, Taranee, and Hay Lin about their powers over the elements, her grandmother had turned to Will and explained about the Heart: a crystal orb that had recently appeared in all the girls' dreams. That was the Heart of Candracar, the uniting force behind the girls' powers.

The orb had been absorbed into Will's body. From that moment on, whenever the Guardians met with trouble, it had reemerged, bursting from Will's palm. Pulsing with power, the Heart helped the girls transform themselves from sweater-and-sneaker-wearing schoolgirls into superstars. They became taller and stronger. Their faces took on knowing, grown-up expressions. Their bodies became curvy, and their clothes morphed into supercool purple-and-turquoise outfits. The best feature of all sprouted from the girls' backs—iridescent, fluttering wings! Even though only Hay Lin could fly, the wings made great accessories!

Finding the open portals had been tricky. Just before she'd passed away, Hay Lin's grandmother had given the girls a magical map of the city. The magical parchment would show the portals to the girls—but only *after* they had been discovered. As the Guardians became more confident in their powers, Hay Lin's grandmother had taken the map away. She'd reached down from her heavenly place in Candracar, plucked the map from Hay Lin's fingers, and caused it to burn to a crisp.

"That map," Hay Lin's grandmother had informed the girls, "was just one step on the road to understanding. Now, think of it no more."

It was hard for them not to think of that map, though. Cornelia wished that she had had it now, to help her find an open portal. She knew that her friends were struggling with the same problem. After leaving Mrs. Rudolph's house, they walked in silence. How were they going to get to Meridian to help Elyon?

Cornelia looked over at Irma; she knew Irma was thinking that the task of saving Elyon was next to impossible.

"Isn't there anything *easier* you could ask us to do?" Irma asked. "You want us to go to Metamoor for Elyon? We're already up to our necks in problems, dealing with what's left of the twelve portals!"

Before Cornelia could snap at Irma that the girls were Elyon's only hope, Will stepped in. She'd been doing that a lot lately. As the Keeper of the Heart of Candracar, she also seemed to be the keeper of the peace.

At first, Cornelia hadn't thought that Will was the best choice for group leader, but recently, Will's leadership had surprised her. Will had been *so* impressive lately that Cornelia had ended up by following her orders. Normally, Cornelia was a girl who liked being the boss almost as much as she liked cool clothes, ice-skating, and having her own cell phone. She was not a follower. When it came to Will, however, Cornelia listened.

"The passageways through the Veil are a secondary problem right now," Will said. "If Meridian exploded, the Veil would be brought down, too. An uprising or war would destroy everything."

Cornelia's eyes widened. It was hard to believe that Elyon—with her impish grin and her shaggy pigtails—could inspire a war! It was true, though. Elyon was so important to

Metamoor that her official title was Light of Meridian.

When Elyon was snatched from Metamoor, Phobos had lost his opportunity to absorb her power and conquer the universe. Instead, he had begun to suck the life from his own world. He'd drained the energy from Meridian's inhabitants, who were a peaceful, simple people, even if they did resemble claw-footed green lizards, red-eyed rhinoceroses, and lumpy, cobalt-colored thugs. Now the Metamoorians lived in medieval squalor. Until Elyon had recently used her magic to obliterate Phobos's horrible prison, they had also lived in fear of being locked away for the slightest transgression against their dictator.

Meanwhile, Phobos was in a gorgeous palace with a magically lush garden. He had transformed many of the garden's flowers into rainbow-colored creatures called Murmurers, who attended to his every need. They told him everything they saw and heard in Metamoor. With the help of the Murmurers, Phobos's army of thugs, and evil henchmen like Cedric, the prince was mighty indeed.

He'd even managed to sell Elyon his lie.

With Cedric's help, Phobos had convinced his sister that her adoptive parents were traitors, not saviors. He made Elyon believe that he'd been searching for her all those years not to destroy her, but to bring her back to her real family, her real home, and now, her throne.

Cornelia agreed with what Mrs. Rudolph had said earlier. Something was fishy about Phobos's willingness to turn over his power. Perhaps he had other plans for Elyon.

Elyon clearly must have had her doubts, too. Why else would she have recently asked the Guardians to help her free her adoptive parents from Phobos's horrible prison?

Yes, Cornelia thought. Elyon is suspicious, but she's not totally convinced that Phobos means her harm.

Cornelia squared her shoulders and pursed her lips in a narrow, tight line.

Taranee's voice interrupted her thoughts. "Let me guess," she said with a sigh. "We're going to take another trip to Monstropolis, right?"

"Sure looks like it," Will said, looking down at the sidewalk. "If only we knew how to get there."

Hay Lin slapped her forehead with her hand. "Without my grandmother's map, we've got a big mess on our hands."

"We could always use the portal in Elyon's basement," Cornelia proposed, referring to the opening that lay at the end of a brick tunnel, deep beneath Elyon's house. "We left it open instead of zapping it closed, remember? Just in case we'd need it again."

"It'll be difficult to get to it without being spotted," Will said, shaking her head. "There are two Interpol agents there, remember?"

"Right!" Irma said irritably. "Those snoops have practically pitched camp at Elyon's place."

"And what if they find out about our secret passageway?" Taranee said, her eyes clouding up with worry behind her big, round glasses.

"No chance," Cornelia said. For the first time that morning, she felt in control of *something*. "I created a magical wall in Elyon's basement. Medina and McTiennan will *never* find the portal underneath it, guaranteed!"

Score one for the earth girl! Cornelia thought happily, as the girls reached their destination—the Sheffield Institute. Together, they walked toward their school's large front stair-case.

"We still have a problem," Irma noted as they climbed the steps. "My dad says those two cops are going to be around for a long time. So, even if *they* can't get to our portal, *we* can't, either!"

Cornelia didn't like to admit it, but Irma did have a point.

"Then, we don't have any other choice," Will agreed. "We have to find a new passage-way to Meridian."

"But that could take us weeks or even months!" Cornelia said. She felt her heart pound more quickly as she imagined Elyon in danger, waiting for them to come to her rescue. "We don't have that much time!"

"If you're talking about the time left for your little chat, Miss Hale, it has definitely run out."

Cornelia froze.

That voice behind her. It was, unmistak-ably—Mrs. Knickerbocker's.

After a quick grimace at her friends, Cornelia turned around. Sure enough, the Sheffield Institute's gray-haired principal was walking toward the girls, her hands clasped sternly behind her back. "Get to class, now, like good students," she ordered Cornelia and her friends. Her voice was cheerful, but it still managed to contain a threatening edge.

"Move along, now, quickly and quietly," Mrs. Knickerbocker continued. "Make your poor principal a happy woman."

"Yes, Mrs. Knickerbocker," Will answered. Before she obeyed, though, she whispered to her friends, "We'll meet up at lunch."

"Yup," Taranee answered for all the Guardians. "Bye, Will."

Great, Cornelia thought as she made her way to her first class. Between the stressful strategy session and Sheffield's cafeteria food, lunch was going to be a pretty unappetizing event.

THREE

Uriah slouched on the front steps of Sheffield Institute. His friends Laurent and Kurt were sitting on either side of him.

I'm the head honcho in this gang, Uriah thought, with a menacing squint at his pals.

Stretching one long, skinny leg out onto the steps, Uriah relaxed. He was happy to be outside, hanging out. So what if he was considered an Outfielder at Sheffield? He didn't mind being on the fringe of the student body. He tripped a few fresh-faced Infielders hurrying into school for their first-period classes.

Snickering at the students, Uriah twisted one of his flame-colored locks into an even spikier spike.

There, Uriah thought with a smirk of

satisfaction. The hierarchy has been reestablished. I totally rule that chunky little Kurt and that big, dumb, jock Laurent. And any bozo who passes by had better sit up and take notice. Because today of all days, I'm in *no* mood for any interference—

"What are you doing out here?"

The voice that had just rung out behind Uriah was deep and forceful.

Hel-*lo*? Uriah complained inwardly. Did I not just say that I was in *no* mood for any interference?

Uriah's squint got squintier as he turned to glare at Mrs. Knickerbocker, who stood before him in her blue suit.

"In case you hadn't noticed," Mrs. Knickerbocker growled once she had Uriah's attention, "the school is *this* way!"

As the principal jabbed a chubby finger toward the building's front door, Kurt spoke up.

"It's our recess time, Mrs. Knickerbocker," he drawled, smiling dully.

Ugh, Uriah thought. Kurt the slush-brain strikes again.

"It's called Physical Education, you troglodyte," he snapped, thwacking Kurt on the back of his big, shaggy head for emphasis.

"Huh-huh-huh!" Laurent guffawed. Uriah turned to Laurent and poked the meathead with his sneaker toe to shut him up. Then he hauled himself to his feet and slunk past the principal into the school's front hall. Kurt and Laurent followed—of course.

I may be obeying the warden, Uriah thought with a sniff, but at least I'm doing it with some 'tude.

"'Troglodyte,'" Mrs. Knickerbocker called after Uriah. "It's so nice to hear you use big words, Uriah. The time you've spent at the museum is starting to pay off!"

"Huh-huh-huh!" Laurent chuckled again.

"I don't think that's funny," Uriah muttered, glancing back at Laurent. Immediately, Laurent's giggly panting turned into a breath-less apology. Uriah shrugged him off. Big, oafish Laurent could cause Uriah, at most, a mere minute's worth of annoyance. Meanwhile, Mrs. Knickerbockers's barbs were good for at least an hour of seething.

"Old mummy!" he spat as he stomped down the hall. "She's the one who should be at the museum: as an exhibit!"

"You know," Kurt piped up from his usual position at Uriah's heels. "That place isn't so bad, after all."

Uriah's sneakers skidded to a halt on the marble floor. He spun around so fast he felt his hair spikes sway. "Shut up, Kurt!" he yelled, grabbing the dork by the front of his fleece. "We were supposed to have gone there for only three months after we broke in looking for those monsters."

Just thinking about the "community service" Judge Cook had ordered the guys to do after they'd broken into the museum made Uriah flush with anger. Could that goody-goody judge *really* tell him that she wouldn't have done the same thing in his shoes? If she'd heard that some talking lizard was slithering around the Heatherfield Museum, dressed up in a suede vest like some gothic peasant, she'd *have had* to check it out.

I was only looking for a learning experience, Uriah smirked as he recalled that night.

Yeah! He should have gotten extra credit instead of being sentenced to hard labor! What's more, his term *should* have been up in ninety days.

"Now, because of you," Uriah continued, thrusting his pointy, oily nose up close to Kurt's stubby one, "we'll be spending a whole year in that place!"

"Be—because of me?" Kurt stuttered. "Why is it always my fault?"

"Who's the one who started playing baseball in the dinosaur hall?" Uriah bellowed.

"I—I was just the batter," Kurt protested. He jerked his head toward Laurent, who was standing off to the side, gazing at the ceiling innocently. "Laurent was the pitcher!"

Laurent waved his arm dismissively—a motion reminiscent of the one he'd used to lob a dinosaur egg through the museum's main exhibit hall. Kurt had gleefully swung at it with a pterodactyl's humerus.

Unfortunately, the museum curator—not to mention Judge Cook—hadn't found their version of baseball very humorous.

So, the gang's sentence had been extended. Well, everyone in the gang except one, that is.

"Nigel's the only one who didn't get in trouble," Laurent complained.

"Oh, he already did his three months and got off clean because he was a *good boy*," Uriah said in a simpering voice. "Yeah, little Nigel's changed. Now he hangs out with 'decent folk,' like Judge Cook's daughter."

"Taranee Cook—*puh!*" Kurt said. "*We* used to be Nigel's friends."

Used to be, Uriah thought. Which means that now he's our enemy. And what happens to our enemies?

Suddenly, Uriah stopped in his tracks. Laurent and Kurt bumped into him with bewildered grunts.

Uriah had an idea. "I propose," he said, index finger to spotty chin, "a little farewell gift for our old friend. What do you say to a nice watch?"

Ignoring his friends' reactions, Uriah began hurrying toward the gym. Looks like we're going to P.E. class after all, he thought.

When the trio arrived at the gym, they peeked through the double doors. Coach O'Neil and a bunch of underclassmen were all gazing upward in morbid fascination. When Uriah craned his neck, too, he almost clapped his hands in delight.

Clutching the climbing rope like a pudgy sloth was David Berlin. The pale-faced, soft-gutted wimp struggled and sweated as he inched up the rope. He was only halfway to the ceiling, and, clearly, the coach wasn't going to grant him clemency.

"Come on, Berlin," the coach yelled at the boy. "You can do it. You're almost there! Come on!"

Actually, he's *not* nearly there, Uriah thought with a wily grin. But *I* am.

Uriah sidled along the gym wall in the direction of the locker room. The coach and students were so absorbed in Berlin's progress that none of them noticed him. Motioning for Laurent to keep watch at the door, Uriah slipped into the locker room with Kurt.

A small mountain of gym bags was heaped on a bench in the center of the room.

Oh, underclassmen, Uriah thought, placing a hand on his heart. I love 'em. They're so naive, so trusting.

Uriah pawed through the bags until he found the nerdiest one—a pale blue, plastic bag, decorated with a little cat and a name tag that said *D. Berlin*.

"Is anyone coming?" Uriah called over his shoulder.

"Not yet," Laurent grunted from his post at the locker-room door.

Uriah unzipped Berlin's bag and fished around inside until his skinny fingers closed around a digital watch with a wide band.

"This should do the trick!" Uriah declared, pulling the watch out of the bag and stashing it inside the pocket of his baggy jeans. He sauntered out of the locker room—a man with a plan.

"I'll catch up with you later," he muttered to his friends. He saw disappointment flash in their eyes. They wanted in on Uriah's brilliant scheme.

Nope! This mission's mine, Uriah thought.

He stole up the staircase, then veered into a hallway lined with lockers. Finally, he reached his destination.

"Here's Nigel's locker," he whispered.

He cupped the lock dangling from the door.

Some kids would be defeated by this obstacle, Uriah thought smugly. But I am not some kids. I actually know his locker combination!

Chuckling, Uriah twirled the dial until he heard a sweet click. He pulled at the lock.

Tlack!

It sprang open.

"Heh-heh!"

Uriah opened the locker with a clatter. He tossed Berlin's goofy watch inside, then slammed the door shut, and scurried back toward the stairwell.

Mission accomplished, he thought sneakily. *And* mission unseen. Oooh, Uriah, you are good! And Nigel, the bully added with a cackle, hope you enjoy the gift.

FOUR

Will walked into the school cafeteria and made a beeline for the dessert cart. Like most Sheffielders, she knew that if she waited until after lunch to make her snack run, all the best choices would be gone. She'd be stuck with fat-free oat bran muffins.

And if I'm going to present my plan to the other Guardians, Will thought, I'm going to need all the energy I can get. This scheme requires sugar.

It was a scheme that had taken Will all morning to concoct. She'd daydreamed through Drama, planned through Math, and scribbled in her notebook during Science.

You know you're not a new kid any-more when you can make it through an entire morning without thinking about actual schoolwork once, Will thought with a giggle. *Funny, only a short time ago, I wanted to be in the know. Then it happened, and I barely noticed.*

When Will had first arrived in Heatherfield and first stumbled into the Sheffield Institute, she'd felt as though she'd *never* get used to that cliff-top city or its sea-scented air, styling student body, and countless crushworthy boys.

Luckily, she'd run into Taranee that first day at school. Taranee had been just as new and just as freaked out as Will was. Soon after that, Cornelia had taken them both under her wing. By Halloween, Will and Taranee had found themselves bonding over silly costumes with Irma, Hay Lin, and Cornelia at the school dance.

A good thing, too, Will thought, juggling her cup of hot chocolate and a big cookie as she headed to her friends' usual table near the window. *After all, it wasn't long afterward that we found out our after-school activities were going to involve saving the world.*

Speaking of which, Will thought, *the gang's all here. It's time to discuss—my plan.*

Will plopped herself down in the last empty chair at the round table. Looking around, she saw that the others had steaming mugs filled with hot chocolate in front of them, too. Irma was shoving aside her sandwich crusts and reaching for a doughnut to dunk into her mug.

The four girls were gazing at Will expectantly, like a platoon of soldiers waiting for their orders, or a classroom full of kids anticipating the next question from the teacher.

Wow, Will thought with raised eyebrows. I guess I've really gotten used to this leadership thing. Maybe I owe it to the Heart of Candracar, floating around inside me.

If that's the case, so be it, Will thought, cheerfully taking a bite of her cookie. I'll need all the power the Heart can give me for this proposal.

Taking a deep breath, Will filled her friends in on what she had in mind. "I've been thinking it over," she announced, "and I might have a solution to our problem."

"You've found a way to get to Meridian?" Taranee asked.

"Yes!" Will said. "We could take the portal that Vathek used to get to Heatherfield a few days ago. Maybe it's still open."

Will still giggled every time she pictured Vathek's arrival at her window that day. Vathek was a giant Metamoorian monster—bright blue and as hefty as a hippopotamus. Once upon a time, he'd been one of Lord Cedric's most vicious henchmen. But when he'd discovered his master's complete lack of honor, he'd defected to the side of the Metamoorian rebels.

One of his first deeds for the good guys had been to come to Heatherfield and find Will. He'd done so by climbing a tree to Will's loft and knocking on her bedroom window! Trying to hide the giant, blue creature from her mom had gotten Will into very hot water.

As if things needed to get *any* tenser with Mom, Will thought with a momentary frown. Ever since Mom started dating—*ewww*—my history teacher, our whole mother-daughter bond has been completely rotten.

Letting Vathek in had turned out to be worth it, though. The creature had brought Will a message—that Elyon needed the Guardians to break her adoptive parents out of Phobos's prison.

He'd also caught a terrible cold during his

Metamoor-to-earth journey. Between his sneezes and his bewilderment at Heatherfield's modern hustle and bustle, he'd been stumped when Will had asked him to lead the Guardians back to his portal.

"When we went back to Metamoor with Vathek," Cornelia pointed out, "we crossed through the portal in Elyon's house."

"Which means that the one Vathek used is still unknown to us," Irma added through a mouthful of doughnut. "In a way, that's good, right? If we haven't found it, we haven't closed it."

"Right," Hay Lin agreed with a shrug of her shoulders. "So where do we think it is?"

"That's the thing," Will said, her own shoulders sagging. "I don't know. But with our powers, it shouldn't be too difficult to find out."

"Want to meet up at my place after school to discuss this?" Taranee offered.

Will nodded as Hay Lin answered quickly, "Count me in!"

"Okay," Cornelia said with a determined frown. "Map or no map, we'll fig—"

Briiiinnnggg!

Will jumped. Had these find-the-portal

negotiations taken the whole lunch period? She hadn't even finished her cookie yet!

"Huh?" Irma said, glancing at her watch in confusion. "The bell's early! We still have ten minutes left."

"Nope," said a passing boy. "Knickerbocker has an announcement to make."

"An announcement!" Irma said. "I think all her so-called authority has finally gone to Knickerbocker's head."

Nevertheless, all five girls got to their feet and hurried out of the cafeteria among a wave of other students. They joined an even larger crowd outside on the school's front steps. Standing on the steps was a pale, wide-eyed boy in a green cardigan and baggy blue jeans. He looked out sadly at the throng of students.

The kid was dwarfed by the woman standing next to him—Mrs. Knickerbocker. The principal was visibly fuming!

"Hmmm!" Cornelia whispered to Will as the girls found a spot in the crowd. "Something must be really wrong. I don't like the look on her face."

As Will nodded, Mrs. Knickerbocker began to speak. "Children, something very serious has happened," she said. "One of you has *truly* disappointed me. Someone has stolen a watch from your classmate David Berlin."

Mrs. Knickerbocker wrapped a protective arm around the boy's shoulders and pulled him to her side. Will could practically hear the boy grunt at the impact.

"Nothing like this has ever happened in my school," the principal continued. "I should call the police to report this incident, but I'm not going to do that. Instead, I hope that the person responsible for this will think carefully about what he or she has done, and will see that the watch is given back to its rightful owner."

Stunned, Will glanced around her. She knew many of these kids. The thought that someone there had stolen something made her supersad.

Clearly, Mrs. Knickerbocker felt the same way. "Now, I'm going to return to my office," she declared, "and you will go straight to your classes. But one thing is certain: I want that watch on my desk by tomorrow morning! I've always had great trust in all of you, and I would like to continue to do so. This is now out of my hands."

Will studied the faces around her.

Who among these Sheffielders, she wondered, is the snake in disguise, just like Cedric?

Will's gaze rested on Martin Tubbs, the supernerd who'd had a crush on Irma for, like, forever. He looked just as shaken as she felt! Especially when Mrs. Knickerbocker uttered her next bit of information.

"And remember, if anyone knows something," she said, "if anyone has seen something and doesn't speak up, they are just as guilty as the thief."

Martin gulped audibly. Will smiled at the kid sympathetically.

Of course, Martin is distressed, she thought. He's Mr. Nice Guy. He probably can't even envision anything as ugly as stealing.

Irma was clearly confused by the disruption in the school day.

"This is crazy!" she said to her friends. "Who could have done it?"

"Nice little mystery, huh?" Hay Lin said with a heavy sigh.

They were just getting ready to head back to their classes when they passed Mrs. Knickerbocker, who was herself at that moment passing by Uriah. The spotty-faced thug was slouching against a locker.

"You wouldn't happen to know anything about this, would you, Uriah?" Principal Knickerbocker asked.

"Hey!" Uriah whined. "Why are you accusing me right off the bat?"

"I'm not accusing you," Mrs. Knickerbocker insisted, "but seeing that you spend more time in the hallways than in the classrooms, you might have noticed something out of the ordinary."

"Yeah, right," Uriah cried. His beady eyes widened.

This was quite an event. Will's friends and dozens of other students stopped to watch the show as well.

"With all due respect, ma'am," Uriah said loudly, "I'm tired of being treated like this. Why don't you have me searched?"

Mrs. Knickerbocker harrumphed and then looked around at the crowd uncomfortably.

"Go on!" Uriah screeched. "Look through my backpack. Open my locker!"

He ran over to a nearby locker that was full of dents and scratches. He began spinning the dial on his combination lock.

"Calm down, Uriah," Mrs. Knickerbocker said. Her voice was full of chagrin. "Don't take it like this."

Uriah ignored the principal, turning instead to Kurt.

"Open yours up, too," he said, pointing at another locker nearby. "'Cause we're the *bad* guys, aren't we? Everything that happens around here is always our fault. So, go ahead, Kurt!"

Uriah turned back to his locker and spun the final digit of his lock. He threw the door open with a *clang*, unleashing a torrent of candy wrappers, old sweat socks, crushed notebooks, and tons of other boy junk.

"Take a look!" Uriah challenged.

Mrs. Knickerbocker covered her mouth with a plump hand, looking shaken. "I didn't mean to offend you," she said as Uriah gazed sadly at his locker contents where they lay strewn on the floor.

Will couldn't help noticing that the pile of junk did not contain a watch.

"Poor Uriah," Irma whispered. "Sure, he can be a first-class brute, but now, I almost feel sorry for him! Though not entirely."

"I apologize," Mrs. Knickerbocker said, putting a hand on Uriah's shoulder, "if you thought that—"

"No, ma'am," Uriah said, shaking off the principal's grip. "If you suspect me, then you have to suspect everyone."

Will narrowed her eyes. Kurt and Laurent squinted, too. But *they* were squeezing their eyes shut in the supreme effort to keep from laughing.

What, Will wondered, is going on here?

"Come on, everyone!" Uriah snarled at the crowd of onlookers. "What are you afraid of? Open up your lockers!"

Will looked around the hallway. Students were giving each other suspicious looks, shuffling their feet, and shrugging uncomfortably.

"Well, I guess . . ." one shaggy-haired dude began to say to a girl standing next to him.

"Come on," she replied with a shrug. Tossing her curls, she loped across the hallway toward her locker.

"Well, all right," another girl said from the center of the crowd.

"Uriah's got a point," a fresh-faced blond

athlete said to no one in particular.

The students in the hall began to drift toward their lockers. Infielders, Outfielders, rebels, jocks—all were ready to prove their innocence.

The first boy to snap open his lock was the coolest kid of all, in Will's humble opinion. That was Matt Olsen, lead singer of Cobalt Blue, *and* her crush of all time. Will found herself holding her breath as Matt swung his locker door open.

His locker contained nothing but a few books and a bag full of guitar picks.

The curly-haired girl's locker was empty, too, except for an impressive array of lip glosses.

Tlack!

The next boy's locker was free of watches.

Tlack! Tlack!

As all the lockers in the hallway slammed open, everyone seemed to be innocent.

Tlack!

Will turned to check out the next locker that was being opened. It belonged to Nigel, Taranee's cute, quiet crush. Will shrugged. Nigel had given up Uriah's lifestyle after he finished his community service sentence and had started hanging out with Taranee. There's no *way*, Will thought, that Nigel's—

Thunk!

Will jumped at the noise. Something had just fallen out of Nigel's locker and landed on the marble floor.

It was a watch.

"That's *my* watch!" David Berlin cried. He scurried around Mrs. Knickerbocker to scoop the timepiece up from the floor.

"Nigel!" Mrs. Knickerbocker gasped, quickly stepping toward him.

"B—but—" Nigel stuttered. He looked from the watch to the principal and back to the watch again. His eyes were wide and bewildered.

"Nigel!" Taranee shouted, before clapping a hand over her mouth. Standing next to Taranee, Will could see shocked tears springing to her friend's eyes. She knew if Taranee took her hand from her mouth, she'd burst into anguished sobs.

"Hold on!" Nigel protested, taking a halting step toward Taranee. "I didn't do it!"

"Oh, Nigel," Uriah said, shaking his head.

"Please come to my office, Nigel," Mrs.

Knickerbocker said in an ominous tone.

Taranee had no words. She could only manage a grief-stricken, choking sound. Will started to put a comforting hand on her friend's shoulder, but before she could make contact, Taranee wheeled around and dashed down the hall.

Will gazed at her classmates' stunned faces. Hay Lin looked shocked. Cornelia shook her head in disgust. Martin seemed strangely guilty. He wrung his hands and turned pale behind his thick glasses.

And me? Will asked herself. How do I feel? Considering that this whole Guardian gig has already got me dizzy, I'd say I'm more confused than ever!

FIVE

Tea, Hay Lin thought as she walked down the hallway of the Cooks' sunny house to Taranee's room. She was balancing a tray laden with clinking cups and a teapot from which aromatic steam wafted.

Tea is just what this moment calls for, she thought. That's what my grandma would say if she were here. When someone needs comforting, you break out the chamomile.

But is tea enough to soothe a broken heart? Hay Lin wondered with a frown. I wouldn't know. I'm still crush-free. And y'know what? I can't say that I'm sorry. After what I've seen recently, having a crush can be tough. Will has been swooning over Matt Olsen practically from the moment she arrived in Heatherfield.

It took him forever to sit up and notice her, and she's still not sure if he likes her. She says it's absolute torture!

As for Cornelia, Hay Lin thought with a sigh, I think I'm going to start calling her Juliet. She even has a star-crossed lover—a Metamoorian rebel named Caleb. I mean, a long-distance relationship can be doable, but having a boyfriend who lives in Meridian's underground and risks his life every day to restore the Light of Meridian? That's impossible. They can't even call each other on the phone!

Before today's horrible watch-in-the-locker fiasco, Hay Lin thought, Taranee's crush had been the most likely to become something sorta real. Taranee *like*-liked Nigel, and he *like*-liked her back. There had been no drama. Taranee had told the Guardians that even Judge Cook was warming up to Nigel.

But as Hay Lin arrived at Taranee's bedroom, the mood was far from romantic or fun. Taranee was slumped against the headboard of her bed, her chin propped morosely on her raised knees. Will and Irma were perched at the foot of the bed, glancing at each other uncomfortably. Cornelia was leaning against the desk, annoyed, no doubt, that Nigel had messed up so badly.

"Tea!" Hay Lin announced in the cheeriest voice she could muster. She skimmed into the room and bustled around, handing cups to each girl. *She* at least found some comfort in the ritual, and, at times like these, any little comfort helped.

Unfortunately, the ritual was all too brief. After a couple of minutes, silence—except for the girls' occasional sullen slurps at their teacups—descended upon the room again.

Somebody, say something, please! Hay Lin thought.

"Taranee?"

Hay Lin looked around the room. The voice was not that of any of the girls.

Taranee's mom had just poked her head through the bedroom door.

"Nigel's on the phone," she said.

Sluggishly, Taranee looked up.

"Oh, really?" she said sarcastically. "Well, I don't want to talk to him. Tell him I'm *not here!*"

"Did something happen?" Judge Cook said, giving her daughter a searching look.

"No, nothing's happened, Mom," Taranee sighed.

Shutting out the parents, Hay Lin noted with a nod. That seems to be another symptom of this whole liking-boys thing. Not that I'm against keeping secrets from your mom and dad, especially when that secret is, oh, the fact that you're a magical being charged with saving the world. Still, lying feels rotten. And it seems you have to do a lot more of it when you're in crush mode!

"Just please tell him I'm not here," Taranee repeated, refusing to meet her mother's eyes.

"As you like," Judge Cook said, slipping out of the bedroom.

The other girls returned to gazing glumly into their teacups.

Hay Lin glanced at Taranee's bedroom door. She looked back at her friends. Inertia would have been too lively a word for their current state.

Finally, Hay Lin rolled her eyes. I guess I have to do all the tea-fetching *and* eavesdropping around here, she thought. She placed her cup on Taranee's desk and slipped out of the room. She had only taken a few steps down the narrow hallway when she heard Judge Cook's voice coming from the living room.

"I—I'm sorry, Nigel," Taranee's mother said a bit awkwardly.

I bet it must be *really* hard for a judge to lie, Hay Lin thought with a cringe.

"But," Taranee's mother went on, "she just left, and—"

Judge Cook's voice was suddenly cut off by Nigel. He was speaking so loudly and angrily that Hay Lin could hear him even though she wasn't holding the phone! Well, she couldn't hear *every* word, but the tone of his voice said it all. Hay Lin knew that he must be insisting he hadn't stolen David Berlin's watch.

"Watch?" Judge Cook said, in confusion. "What are you talking about? Nigel? Hello? *Nigel?*"

He must have hung up, Hay Lin thought.

Shaking her head, Hay Lin returned to Taranee's bedroom. Things there had definitely livened up a bit. But not in a good way.

Taranee was sitting on the edge of her bed, her face buried in her hands. She was crying, while Will rubbed her back, looking distressed.

"Cheer up, Taranee," she pleaded gently.

"Don't take it so hard. Please?"

Taranee shook her head. "I just can't believe it," she sobbed. "I don't *want* to believe it."

"But we all saw it with our own eyes," Cornelia reminded her from across the room.

"Thanks for the encouragement, Cornelia," Irma said drily.

Taranee sobbed more. The sound stabbed Hay Lin in the heart, bringing tears to her own eyes. She took a step toward her friend. At the same time, Irma and Cornelia moved forward. Instinctively, the Guardians formed a tight circle around their friend, trying to bring back some cheer.

It was a useless effort. Not even the Power of Five could improve Taranee's mood at that moment. With her head still bowed, Taranee whispered, "Could we—could we just change the subject, please?"

"Sure, Taranee," Will said quietly. She looked over at Hay Lin desperately.

Right, Hay Lin thought. Subject change, subject change. Change of subject, huh? How is it that I can think of a million things I'm dying to say during biology class, but now, when I need to speak, my mind is a blank?

As she pondered, Hay Lin dug her hands into the pockets of her jeans.

Click.

Her fingernail had hit something in her pocket.

"Hey!" she announced. "I think I've found a way to locate the portal that Vathek used!"

"Really?" Cornelia cried, leaving the mournful circle around Taranee to clap Hay Lin on the back. "That would be the first piece of good news we've had in weeks!"

"But how?" Taranee asked quietly, wiping the tears from her cheeks.

"With this!" Hay Lin said. She pulled a flat, round object out of her pocket and held it up for her friends to see. It was a token, about the size of a quarter. "Remember when Will and Vathek snuck Cornelia past those nosy Interpol agents a few days ago?" Hay Lin asked.

"So we could go to Metamoor to rescue Elyon's adoptive parents," Will acknowledged with a nod.

"Uh-huh," Hay Lin replied. "And you used the pet-shop van as your getaway car."

"Ugh, don't remind me," Will said, with an

uneasy grin. "Creating a double of Mr. Olsen to drive the van was a crazy scheme. I still get carsick when I think about it!"

"Well, it's a good thing it was such a rocky ride!" Hay Lin said. "This token fell out of Vathek's pocket. And since one of my powers is being able to read the memories of sounds trapped in inanimate objects, this piece of metal should tell me where it came from."

"And when we find that out," Will said, hopping to her feet, "we'll also know where Vathek crossed through the Veil. Great idea, Hay Lin!"

"Come on, admit it," Irma said. "Someone gave you that idea."

"You're just jealous, Irma," Hay Lin retorted with a sly grin. "Now, be quiet. I have to concentrate."

A breathless hush filled the room as Hay Lin dropped the token on Taranee's hardwood floor.

The coin hit the surface with a flat little *tling!* At least, that's how it sounded to Hay Lin at first. When she closed her eyes, though, the *tling* turned into more of a chiming sound.

The chime then morphed into a vision. A

beautiful vision of a mystical realm filled with floating prisms and crystals.

Hay Lin held out her hands, to steady herself on Taranee's desk chair. Or was it Will's supportive shoulder? She didn't know, exactly. It was hard to stay connected to her body when her mind was careening through space. Hay Lin felt as if she were catapulting through velvety water. Sparkling crystals whizzed past her like asteroids.

Each one of those sparkly prisms was infused with sound. Hay Lin could feel the noises more than hear them. As a laughter-infused crystal rushed past her, she felt ticklish all over.

A prism filled with excited shouts made her belly feel light, as if she'd just completed a beautiful drawing.

The next sound was that of a whirring machine. It filled Hay Lin's nose with the phantom scent of warm sugar.

Hay Lin was enjoying these sounds so much it took her a moment to notice something. The crystals—those tiny, mineral-like distillations of sound—were not actually flying past her.

She was plunging through *them*!

She was traveling through a tunnel made of language and laughter and rustling leaves. And if Hay Lin had learned anything from her travels between Heatherfield and Meridian, it was that every tunnel had an end.

This one ended in a square of light.

Going toward the light? Hay Lin thought. Isn't that usually the wrong way to go?

Even if it were, there was no time to turn back. Hay Lin was flying toward that square.

Whoooooossssh!

She plunged into the light.

The crystals and prisms disappeared, as did the empty black space in which they'd been floating.

Now, it was Hay Lin who was floating. She was in a murky place where she could see little but could smell everything. She detected sawdust and peanuts and . . . cotton candy! That was the warm, sugary stuff she'd smelled in the tunnel.

Hay Lin's eyes began to focus again. A smear of red suddenly became a bobbling, red balloon. A toddler sitting on his father's shoulders was clutching the string. Nearby, other parents and kids wandered about. They were walking away from a Ferris wheel. And there was a roller coaster, and a haunted house whose facade was a giant witch's face.

Just as Hay Lin felt she had gotten her bearings, the scene melted away.

She found herself in another dark tunnel. Instead of otherworldly prisms, the tunnel was furnished with more earthly stuff, like rusty subway tracks and curved walls covered with peeling paint.

This tunnel had the stale light and musty scent of a place long abandoned. But it did have one visitor. Hay Lin saw his shadow first; it loomed, very large indeed, against the wall.

When the visitor emerged from the tunnel, Hay Lin let out a happy gasp.

He was huge. He was blue. He was Vathek.

Almost against her will, Hay Lin's eyes flapped open. Her vision—so tangible a moment ago—evaporated into a wispy haze. Now Hay Lin was back with her friends, who were all looking at her expectantly.

"Of course," Hay Lin said. "Now I get it! It's an amusement park—the old abandoned carnival grounds just outside Heatherfield!"

"Are you sure?" Will asked.

"Totally!" Hay Lin declared. She scooped the token up from the floor and gazed at it. "I bet this was a token for the target-shooting booth."

"I don't know why Vathek picked this up," Will said, plucking the token from Hay Lin's palm, "but he sure did us a big favor!"

Hay Lin felt a happy glow flow through her.

Maybe I don't know how it feels to have a crush, she thought, but I do have feelings that can be very powerful.

Clearly, Cornelia agreed. Reaching out to give Hay Lin's hand an excited squeeze, she declared, "At this point, all that's left for us to do is go back to Meridian!"

SIX

Elyon sat on her balcony, a shell-shaped platform that jutted out from Phobos's giant palace and provided an incredible view of Meridian. A looming archway, with swaying curtains of green velvet, led from the balcony to Elyon's bedchamber.

The chair in which Elyon sat was upholstered in plush blue silk, and its arms were gold. It looked more like a throne than like an ordinary chair.

How appropriate, Elyon thought somewhat sadly. If I'm going to become Metamoor's queen tomorrow, I suppose I should get used to such a seat, even if it isn't nearly as comfy as my old beanbag chair at home.

As the word *home* flitted across her

mind, Elyon shook her head impatiently.

When am I going to realize, she thought, that *this* is my home? Metamoor is my destiny. I'm meant to be the Light of Meridian, not some Heatherfield schoolgirl. That's why my brother is going to so much trouble to throw me this big coronation.

Speaking of which, she thought as she surveyed the always-gray Metamoorian sky, I wonder what will happen at this big ceremony. Shouldn't somebody tell me what need to do? Shouldn't I be working on a speech or learning some crazy incantation?

"Princess!"

Elyon jumped at the sound and peeked over her shoulder. Emerging from one of the green curtains, like a shadow come to life, was a creature that matched the dark green of the curtains. The creature's limbs were long and spiky, and her hair was as white as dandelion fluff. Her exclamation had sounded like a whisper—raspy and ethereal.

Hmmm, ask and ye shall receive, Elyon thought drily. I swear, Murmurers can read my thoughts!

"You'll catch a cold in this draft," the

Murmurer hissed, clinging like a lizard to the curtain.

"The wind doesn't bother me, Murmurer," Elyon said haughtily, silently adding, As if you care.

"Why don't you rest awhile?" the creature suggested, peeking around the high back of her chair with unnervingly twitchy movements. "Tomorrow is going to be a big day, and you will need all of your energy."

"Nonsense," Elyon said. "Where's my brother? I've been waiting to speak to him all day!"

"The prince is very busy, Your Highness," the Murmurer said. "The ceremony of passing down the crown of Meridian requires long purification rites—"

"Sure," Elyon snapped, cutting the creature off rudely. The slimy little thing irked Elyon so much that she suddenly had a strange urge, one that forced her to curl her hands into fists and clench every muscle in her body.

Elyon quickly turned her back on the creature. She found herself staring at the green velvet curtains in rage. Stretching her arms out, she used her magic to push the drapes. The fabric billowed and fluttered in the air.

As long as Phobos is still in charge, Elyon fumed, all I can do is keep quiet and wait, just as I've done every day since I arrived here. From that moment on, all Phobos has done is avoid me. He's more like a stranger than a brother.

Elyon clung to the curtain as she gazed out at the endless city that she was somehow supposed to rule.

I have a million questions to ask Phobos about this city, she thought, and about how he's ruled over it all these years.

Once again, Elyon felt her mood shift back to anger. Wistful sadness to pent-up rage seemed to be her entire emotional range these days. And it seemed as if rage were winning out.

For all my questions, Elyon thought with a grimace, I still haven't gotten any answers. But tomorrow, I'll *demand* them.

That, in the end, Elyon thought with narrowed eyes, is a queen's right.

SEVEN

Cedric felt a bit breathless. He always did when he was face-to-face with Prince Phobos. He felt honored now, as he stood with Phobos in the room that held the prince's greatest secret—and source of his power. The room—built into the peak of the palace's tallest turret—had five walls, all carved from blue stone. Each wall had one porthole-shaped window; none of the windows had glass in them.

Glass would have obstructed the flow of pure, magic energy. The bright, fluorescent-yellow river of light that moved through the room was the purest, most powerful force in all of Meridian.

Cedric gazed at the intense light pouring through the turret's windows. It flowed like golden liquid down the walls, then streamed across the floor. Finally, the five rivers of sunlight converged in a large basin, a cauldron shaped like a giant flower. In that cauldron, the light was converted into magic energy, a burbling source of power unlike any other.

Surrounding the center were three large marble statues of fists, which loomed over the room. Each fist held a giant crystal orb. Three Murmurers stood by, guarding this center of power and light.

Cedric smiled. Ah, Elyon, he thought. These past months, he'd quite enjoyed instructing her to follow Phobos blindly. As he turned her against her earthly friends and coaxed her into Phobos's thrall, she'd been clay in his hands—well, at least until recently, when she'd had a few minor rebellious impulses.

All right, Cedric admitted to himself. Throwing a tantrum that set off an earthquake had been more than a minor instance of rebellion. Elyon had managed to obliterate the Meridian prison pretty handily, too.

Still, Cedric told himself, she is no match for our prince.

Nodding emphatically, he cleared his mind

of the troubling images of his young charge, and again gazed at his master, Phobos.

"Elyon has good cause to be nervous," the prince was saying. "In a few hours, my sister will address the people of Meridian, yet it will be only to say, 'Adieu.'"

Phobos turned toward Cedric. Immediately, Cedric's breathlessness returned. He pushed his long, blond hair back behind his ears.

"You'll be there at her side," Phobos informed Cedric, as he continued to explain his plan. "As master of ceremonies, you will accompany Elyon to the coronation."

"And then what will happen, my lord?" Cedric inquired respectfully.

"Then," Phobos declared with a cackle, "there will be an end to all of this! Look around you, Cedric. Here, a river of magic energy once flowed."

Almost wistfully, Phobos dipped a hand in the cauldron, bathing his fingers in golden magic.

"It was the purest and most powerful source in all of Meridian," he continued. "I used this energy to become stronger, to take over entire worlds."

Phobos withdrew his hand. It was still glowing as he held it before his handsome face, but it dimmed a bit when he uttered his next words.

"Those fools in Candracar thought they could punish me for those acts by cutting me off from the rest of the universe with their ridiculous Veil," Phobos spat angrily. "I won't say it worked. But the power that once flowed in abundance into this turret did become a mere trickle. With each passing day, this world came closer and closer to perishing."

Cedric bowed his head. The notion of his master's being conquered made him tremble with rage. Or was it fear?

Cedric didn't, however, have time to contemplate such matters in detail. Prince Phobos was speaking again.

"Elyon's return," he announced, "changed many things. She is the Light of Meridian!"

As Phobos spoke, two Murmurers entered the chamber. Unusually muscular for their kind, the amphibious creatures were dragging a large trunk across the floor. The box was elaborately decorated, inlaid with gold and mother-of-pearl.

Phobos glanced at the creatures, sending

them a telepathic order to open the trunk quickly. Blinding white light flowed from the chest! It was even brighter than the light of the magic in the cauldron. Cedric had to shield his eyes as Phobos continued to speak.

"Elyon has yet to realize the extent of her limitless powers," he informed Cedric. "That is why, tomorrow, I will be able to take her power for my own. After the long search for my sister, she and her magic will be *mine*!"

"Ah!" Cedric cried, finally understanding. He could not help exulting in his master's devious plan. When Phobos became king, Cedric's own position would be elevated. "The Light of Meridian," Cedric declared joyously, "is about to go out forever!" But then Cedric had a thought that cast a shadow over Phobos's plan. "But how will you manage to take over Elyon's powers?"

"With this, Cedric!" Phobos declared. He reached into the ornate trunk. For a moment, his slender hands were swallowed up by the bright, swirling magic. When they emerged, they held a delicate crown of a silvery platinum color. The front of the crown held a large and brilliant purple gem.

"This is the Crown of Light," Phobos said.

"Using the residual magical energy of Meridian, I will create a trap capable of harnessing Elyon's forces."

Phobos crossed the room, his silken robes fluttering around him. With due ceremony, he dunked the crown into the cauldron. The liquid magic inside the large basin flowed over the precious metal with an ominous sizzle.

"When I place this crown on Elyon's head, it will absorb her powers," Phobos said, his voice trembling ever so slightly with the effort of preparing the magical infusion. "With Elyon's energy at my disposal, I will finally destroy the Veil. I will once again be free!"

Phobos unleashed an evil laugh that lasted until the fiery sounds from the basin subsided. The crown was ready. The prince lifted the delicate crown out of the basin. It pulsated with magic.

"You," Phobos said, addressing the crown almost tenderly, "will deal with my sister and free me from her presence, once and for all!"

As Phobos's words rang out against the chamber's stone walls, Cedric sensed a rustling in the room. He glanced at the Murmurers. They were shifting on their webbed feet, clasping and unclasping their hands. Their eyes rolled backward as knowledge flowed into their heads.

The Murmurers are Phobos's eyes and ears, Cedric noted silently. They see, hear, and feel all that occurs in Meridian. And I have a feeling I know just what is flowing through their simple minds right now.

"Your Highness," Cedric said, as gently as possible. "The entire city will be in the square to witness the ceremony. Your sister is greatly loved! How will the people of Meridian react?"

"That will be no concern of ours!" Phobos spat, hunching forward to cradle the crown closer to his chest.

Cedric wanted to accept Phobos's answer blindly, faithfully. But he had seen what the rebels of Meridian were capable of and had observed the force of their convictions. Cedric took a deep breath before approaching the prince. "Forgive me my insolence, Your Highness," Cedric said, choking, "but I do not think that your army will be strong enough to fight off the crowd."

Cedric braced himself for the *zap* of one of the Murmurers' sparkling spears: a quick, painful punishment ordered from the depths of Phobos's mind.

Instead, the prince barely looked at him. He was too busy gazing eagerly at the chamber's largest door.

Thump, thump, thu-ump.

From a distance, Cedric heard the sound of feet hitting a stone floor in perfect unison.

"I've already thought of the possibility of revolt," Phobos assured his servant. "If it does break out, my *new* Murmurers will deal with them.

Thump, thump, THUMP.

The footsteps were coming closer now. Cedric felt his breath grow shorter, fluttering within his chest like a terrified bird.

Phobos placed a hand on Cedric's shoulder and guided him to the chamber door, which opened into a long, stone corridor. Cedric followed his master's gaze down the corridor. Despite himself, he gasped—as Phobos smiled with satisfaction.

"Observe, Cedric," he said, "and learn to fear them."

Cedric's jaw dropped as he gazed at row upon row of stern-faced creatures with bulging muscles. Their armored chests were wide, and their fists big enough to crush boulders. They had grotesque faces and white eyes, which stared blankly through red masks. They were expressionless, yet more menacing than anything Cedric had ever encountered.

"Learn," Prince Phobos told his now-quaking assistant, "to fear my army of Annihilators!"

EIGHT

Irma looked past her nose at the rusty chain-link fence and gazed at the ripped up roller coaster tracks, the motionless merry-go-round, and the decrepit Ferris wheel of the old Heatherfield carnival.

Look at that roller coaster! The Sooper Screamer! When I was little I loved it, Irma sighed with a dreamy, lopsided smile. But my friends and I are not here for amusement-park rides.

"So," Will said, bringing Irma back to the present. She and the other Guardians were leaning against the carnival fence. But none of *them* had dreamy, lopsided smiles on their faces. They were thinking about the task at hand.

"Should we get going?" Will asked.

As Will reminded her of their mission, Irma groaned.

This is too ironic, she thought. As much as I yearned to go to this carnival when I was a kid, that's how much I'd like to avoid it right now! The kind of roller coaster ride that awaits us in there—a plunge through a portal, straight to Metamoor—is going to be no fun at all! I know it's a Guardian's job—ready to heed the call and all—but truthfully, I'd love an excuse to put off this little trip—at least until after tonight's episode of *Boy Comet*. Sigh.

Brrrippp! Bripppp!

"Oops!" Will said, reaching into the pocket of her gray hoodie to pull out her vibrating cell phone.

"Hello?" she said into the phone as the other Guardians shot each other quizzical glances. "It's me. Yeah, she's right here! I'll put her on."

Will handed the phone over to Irma. "It's for you," she said. "It's Martin!"

"You're kidding, right?" Irma gasped.

Okay, this day is getting stranger and stranger, Irma thought as she took the phone from Will. I mean, sure, things have changed between me and Martin lately. Used to be, he adored me, thought of me constantly, sent me love notes, and greeted me with sickeningly sweet sayings like, "Hello, my little doughnut." *I*, in turn, treated Martin like dirt. It wasn't a particularly balanced system, but, hey, it seemed to work for us. Then one day, Martin surprised me by turning out to be, well, not *quite* as dorky as I'd thought. After we'd had a "date" at the Heatherfield Museum, you could even say we became friends.

But that doesn't mean I want to have a nice, long chat with him when I'm about to risk my life in Metamoor, Irma complained silently. Martin's nerd factor may have improved, but his timing hasn't!

"What do you want, Martin?" Irma blustered into the phone. "I'm really busy and—"

Martin interrupted with a frenetic string of SAT words.

Irma heaved a deep, irritated sigh. This was *so* typically Martin. It would take him an hour to get to his point! She was just about to cut him off—when something he said caught her attention.

Something important.

"*What?*" Irma cried, in response. "Are you serious?"

When Martin answered in the affirmative, using as many syllables as humanly possible, Irma said, "Okay. We'll meet you over at the Golden in half an hour."

A half hour later, Martin and the Guardians were digging in to a pizza at the Golden, one of Irma's fave diners. Irma felt a little guilty. The Guardians had had to ditch their Metamoor trip in order to talk to Martin.

She grinned guiltily as she grabbed a slice of the pizza Martin had ordered before the girls arrived. It was covered with pepperoni.

At the moment, Martin had all of the girls' attention. He was about to tell them about something more pressing, if possible, than pizza.

"So, then your folks said you were out with Will," Martin was explaining to Irma, who sat next to him in a long booth. "I called Will's place, and her mom gave me the number of her cell—"

"Whatever, Martin!" Irma interrupted.

When Martin's face fell, Irma impulsively squeezed his arm. Even she sensed how hard it must have been for him to call the girls together like that. She knew she needed to be more understanding. "Begin at the beginning, and tell us everything you know."

Martin took a deep breath and pushed his thick glasses farther up on his pug nose.

"I really wanted to tell you everything at school," he began. "But, well, I was scared."

Then Martin fell silent, as if he couldn't find the right words to say what he needed to say.

"Of what?" Will prompted gently.

Martin ducked his head and stared into his soda. "Nigel had nothing to do with the watch theft," he finally declared, all in a rush. "It was Uriah who stole David Berlin's watch. I saw him!"

"What?" the Guardians cried in unison.

"*When* did you see him?" Hay Lin asked.

Martin loosened up a bit. He put a stubby finger to his temple and said, "Well, this is what happened. I was on my way to see Mrs. Knickerbocker, and I was thinking to myself, this beats everything. I was kicked out of class because I studied *too much*."

Irma snorted.

"It's crazy," Martin said, looking befuddled. "These days, answering questions has become a crime. I can't help it if I raise my hand before the others do. My arm just shoots up all by itself."

Martin demonstrated, throwing one skinny arm straight up into the air. "It's got a mind of its own," Martin went on. "Maybe I should see a neurologist—"

"Martin!" Irma cried.

Martin shut his mouth abruptly and blinked at Irma.

"Uriah and the watch," she said, reminding him.

"Oh! Oh, yeah," Martin said. "So, it was that simple. I was walking down the hall, thinking about my misbehaving arm, when all of a sudden, I turned a corner and saw Uriah breaking into Nigel's locker. He put David Berlin's watch inside the locker, slammed it shut, and stomped away, muttering all sorts of mean things under his breath."

"But, why didn't you say so right away?" Taranee cried. She was so distressed she was squeezing her pizza crust into a ball.

"And have to go up against Uriah and his thugs?" Martin squeaked. "Those guys don't kid around. But I can't let an innocent person take the blame, either."

He twisted around in his squeaky vinyl seat to face Irma. "What should I do?" he asked.

"What do you think?" Irma asked breezily. She had to admit she felt slightly less than breezy inside. Martin was dead right about Uriah. He could mess Martin up so bad he'd be unrecognizable!

But if Martin stays quiet, Nigel could get into major trouble! Irma thought melodramatically. Which would make Martin feel horrible.

Irma didn't want to see that happen.

"Tomorrow morning," Irma declared lightly, "you go straight to Mrs. Knickerbocker and tell her everything."

Martin rubbed his head, making his hair even more tousled than it had been before. "Yeah, right," he said morosely. "And then what'll happen to me?"

Across the table, Cornelia and Taranee exchanged sly glances. "What are you talking about?" Cornelia said. "We'll protect you!"

"*Sure,*" Martin said sarcastically. "And

who's going to protect you?"

"Oh, we know how to defend ourselves," Hay Lin added, flexing her biceps with a smile.

"My mom, after all," Taranee said, "is a judge, and my dad's a lawyer."

"And *my* father's a cop!" Irma volunteered.

"If I talk," Martin said, plunking his chin down onto his folded arms, "what I'm going to need is a doctor. Does anyone have a relative who works in a hospital? I'd even settle for a second cousin! Because when Uriah and his pals are done with me, my face is going to look like this pepperoni pizza."

Irma couldn't help herself. "So what's the worry?" she quipped, punching Martin's arm. "No one will notice the difference."

Martin tried to laugh, but all he could muster was a scared grimace.

"I was hoping to get some good advice," he sighed as he pulled himself to his feet.

"And we just gave it to you," Irma insisted. "You take care of talking with the principal, and we promise, nobody will hurt you! Do you trust us, or don't you?"

The next morning, Irma and her friends had

their answer. Well, Irma had hers, anyway. She was peeking through Principal Knickerbocker's window, which was about eight feet off the ground. The other Guardians were just below her, boosting her up so she could see what was happening inside.

The scene was enough to send shivers down any school kid's spine. Martin and Nigel were seated in two high-backed, very uncomfortable-looking chairs. With much gesturing and many multisyllabic words, Martin was recounting Uriah's devious scheme to a stony-faced Mrs. Knickerbocker.

Finally, Martin finished his tale. "That's all, ma'am," he said, exhaling deeply.

"Hmmm, I see," the principal grumbled.

Irma held her breath. Did ol' Knickerbocker believe Martin? Or was Irma going to have to protect him from the principal, after all?

"You're a fine young man, Martin," Mrs. Knickerbocker said finally.

Whew! Irma thought with relief.

"I can imagine how difficult it must have been for you to tell me all of this," she went on. She turned to Nigel.

"I wanted you to hear this as well, Nigel,"

she said. "I think you've found a new friend."

"Thanks, Martin!" Nigel whispered to the grinning boy. Irma couldn't help feeling a little pride. And Martin was beaming.

But wait a minute. Why is Knickerbocker staring into the corner? Irma pushed herself further up on the window ledge to get a better view of the principal's office.

"Is there anything you'd like to add, *Uriah*?" Mrs. Knickerbocker asked icily.

Irma gasped as Uriah slunk out of the shadow in the corner. He'd been there the whole time, which meant Martin was totally outed!

At the moment, though, it was Uriah who was in the hot seat.

"It was only a joke, ma'am," he said, stuttering. "It was just for a laugh."

"Well, I hope you've enjoyed yourself," Mrs. Knickerbocker said, "because your little prank is going to cost you five days of suspension!"

"Yes!" Irma whispered, pumping her fist. She pumped so hard, in fact, that her friends lost their grip, and she had to jump to the ground below Mrs. Knickerbocker's office window. "They're leaving the office! Let's go!" she cried, once she was safely back on the ground.

The girls ran inside and skidded to a halt around the corner from Mrs. Knickerbocker's office. They'd arrived just in time. As they peeked around the corner and cocked their heads, the principal escorted the boys out into the hallway.

"Later on," she was telling them, "I'll make an announcement to explain to everyone what happened. Oh, one last thing, Uriah."

All three boys stopped trudging away and paused to look back at Mrs. Knickerbocker.

"This whole thing ends right here," Mrs. Knickerbocker ordered Uriah sternly. "If *any-thing* should happen to Martin, and you know what I mean, I will be *extremely* angry."

"Oh!" Uriah said with a high-pitched and very fake laugh. "No problem, ma'am. I prom-ise."

Martin, sweet guy that he was, actually believed Uriah. He strode over to the bully, who was at least two heads taller than he, and stuck out his hand for a shake. "What do you say we let bygones be bygones, Uriah?" he said, with a slight quiver in his voice.

"Sure thing, pal!" Uriah said loudly.

But then, Irma and her friends noticed something as Mrs. Knickerbocker turned her back. It looked as though Uriah were squeezing Martin's hand so hard that the smaller boy's knuckles went white. Uriah gritted his teeth and leaned in to mutter something to Martin. Irma couldn't hear the entire exchange, but she did catch some phrases like "Say bye-bye!" and "Goner" and "After school, you worm!" Those words were enough to prove that Uriah was issuing a threat!

When he'd finished, Uriah let go of Martin's hand and stalked off.

"Everything okay, Martin?" Nigel asked, shaking his head at the departing bully.

"Oh, sure," Martin said, though he was visibly quaking. "Things couldn't be better."

For Taranee, at least, those words were actually true! The moment Mrs. Knickerbocker slammed her office door shut, she burst out from the Guardians' hiding place.

"Nigel!" she cried, running toward him. "I'm so happy this whole thing is over!"

Nigel looked over at Taranee and nodded

with a sweet and totally goofy smile.

Ah, young love, Irma thought.

"For me it's all over," Nigel told Taranee, "but Martin's in a heap of trouble. Uriah must have threatened him."

Irma's crooked smile evaporated as she watched Martin move down the hallway. He was a quivering mess. With Will, Cornelia, and Hay Lin in tow, Irma ran after him.

"Martin!" Will said when they'd caught him. "Don't worry about that creep."

"It doesn't matter, guys," Martin said, squaring his bony shoulders with false bravery. "I thought about it over and over again, and I'm sure I did the right thing. Talking about it with you really helped me out. I saw how sure you were about it, and I understood that I shouldn't be afraid of facing up to things."

You could say that about a lot of things, Irma realized, biting her lip and thinking about the carnival she'd been so eager to ditch.

"I'm going to work this one out on my own!" Martin continued. "And if Uriah breaks my glasses, no big deal. It wouldn't be the first time it's happened, and it probably won't be the last."

Then he took off his glasses and began polishing them. With a firm nod, he stalked off down the hall. Well, staggered down the hall is more like it. Without his specs, he was blind as a bat.

He was also, Irma had to admit, a friend to be proud of.

"Martin is a whole lot braver than I thought," Cornelia whispered to the other Guardians.

"But we won't let him go through this alone," Will said. Instinctively, Irma and the others gathered around her as she issued a plan.

"Before we leave for Meridian," the Guardians' leader declared, "we're going to see this through!"

NINE

As Will walked out of the school with her friends, she felt buoyant. She loved the idea of rescuing Martin from that bully, Uriah.

Her friends, however, were a little worried.

"When we haven't transformed," Hay Lin whispered urgently, "our powers aren't at their top levels."

"But they're more than enough to take care of Uriah and his pals," Irma said. She said it, however, with considerably *less* confidence than she'd displayed to Martin a few minutes earlier.

"Whatever we do," Cornelia insisted, "we just have to make sure we're not seen."

Cornelia didn't sound scared. She sounded tense and thoroughly ill-tempered. By now, though, Will knew how to translate that tone: Cornelia was feeling just as apprehensive as her friends.

Well, just wait until I tell them about my secret weapon! Will thought.

With a smile, she announced, "Don't worry, Cornelia. We'll use a little trick I discovered not too long ago. Something called . . ."

Just before she let the cat out of the bag, Will stopped herself. She decided to show her friends instead of telling them.

With that, she clenched her fists, closed her eyes, and turned her attention inward, to the beating of her heart and the magic of the Heart of Candracar welling up inside her.

Will felt jets of pink magic suffuse her body. Normally, that phenomenon made Will feel stronger, sharper, and more solid in every way. But today, she was going for the opposite effect, namely . . .

"Invisibility," Will announced with satisfaction when her transformation was complete. She opened her eyes just in time to see her friends' faces blanch as her body shimmered away into nothingness.

"Wow!" Irma squeaked.

"You said it," Will replied, holding her hands out in front of her to admire her body's not-thereness. "I just discovered this power the other day. Let me explain how it works."

Within a few minutes, all five of the Guardians had disappeared—at least to the eyes of any fellow Sheffielders who might have been around. Once they were safely invisible, they pressed themselves against the fence that surrounded the school grounds and watched their classmates pour onto the sidewalk shouting good-byes, digging through backpacks, or grubbing last-minute rides home.

Finally, the student the Guardians were waiting for tromped through the gates. He was skinny. His blond hair was parted in the middle, and his thick glasses were sitting on the edge of his nose. Martin Tubbs was a moving geek target.

And, boy, did he seem to know it. As she watched him walk past the Guardians, Will could see beads of sweat rolling down Martin's cheeks. His hand gripping his backpack's strap was white-knuckled. Every noise he heard, whether it was a chipmunk scrabbling in the leaves or a car beeping its horn, made him jump and scan the sidewalk. He looked certain that he was being watched.

Oh, you are, Martin, Will thought with a grin. She and her invisible friends were right behind him.

And they weren't the only ones.

"Pssst! Martin!"

Will tensed. The voice was coming from a gateway in a tall, brick wall that Martin had just passed.

"If it's me you're looking for," the voice hissed, "here I am!"

"U—Uriah!" Martin squeaked.

Perfect, Will thought. He's not even a block away from Mrs. Knickerbocker's office!

Uriah pushed himself off the wall and slung his arm around Martin's neck. Casually, he held the smaller kid in a choke hold and dragged him into a park a few feet away. While Martin trembled in Uriah's grip, Kurt and Laurent ambled out from behind the wall. They guffawed as Uriah grinned and said, "I gave you my word, Martin. And you know me—I'm a guy who keeps his promises. I never stand people up, right, Kurt?"

"Uh-huh," Kurt, the portly sidekick, confirmed with a chuckle. He pulled a little notebook out of his jeans pocket. "You even wrote it down in your appointment book, Uriah. Two o'clock P.M. to two-thirty P.M. . . . 'Beat up Martin.'"

Uriah glanced at his watch and shook his head.

"Gosh, it's already twenty past," he said to his whimpering captive. He released Martin from the choke hold and grabbed him by the front of his windbreaker—the better to glare straight into the kid's eyes.

"If you want, Martin, we can reschedule for another day," Uriah growled. "Sure! What do you say to Friday, same time? Now that I'm *suspended*, I have lots of free time."

"But it's not my fault," Martin choked. "I couldn't pretend like nothing happened and let Nigel get in trouble!"

"Well, you'd have been better off letting him," Uriah snarled, shaking Martin violently. "Now, tomorrow, if anyone asks what happened to you, just tell them you fell down the stairs!"

Martin covered his horrified face with his

hands. "Wait, Uriah," he pleaded. "Let's talk this over!"

But Uriah was *not* in a talking mood. He made a fist.

Martin cringed and braced himself for the beating of his life! He kept waiting and then . . .

Plonk!

"Ow!" Uriah cried. A pinecone had just bonked him in the head! He dropped Martin's jacket to rub his gluey red spikes with his hands.

"Who—who did that?" he demanded, looking at Kurt and Laurent.

"Nobody," Kurt drawled, pointing over his head. "It just fell from that tree!"

Just fell? Oh, I don't think so! Will thought smugly. Unbeknownst to those boys, she'd been watching the entire sordid scene from just a few feet away. More important, *Irma* had been watching, too, from up in the pine tree! Looking up at the tree's lowest branch, Will saw another pinecone floating in the air.

"Come on!" Irma whispered to Will from her perch. "Can't I throw another one at him? Just one?"

"No, Irma!" Will whispered back with a

giggle. "There are five of us. You don't want to hoard all the fun for yourself, do you?"

"Oh, man," Irma complained with a chuckle. "You're no fair."

Will was prepping a snappy comeback of her own when Laurent cried, "Hey!"

Will jumped and turned back to the boys. Four had become three. Martin had made a break for it! He was sprinting into the park.

"The creep is getting away!" Laurent grunted.

"Get him!" Uriah ordered his flunkies.

"Okay, ladies!" Will announced. "It's our turn! Let's give these bullies the lesson they deserve!"

"Say no more," Cornelia whispered.

As the thugs raced after Martin, Will saw a stream of green magic form, as if out of thin air. It was Cornelia's earth power! Just as Kurt ran beneath the tree, Cornelia's magic made a tree branch suddenly come to life, thwacking Kurt right in the face.

"Ugh!" he grunted as he fell on his back. He stayed on his back, too, moaning and groaning.

Even though he was thoroughly confused by Kurt's case of tree whiplash, Laurent didn't bother to stop. He kept running.

"Nice shot!" Cornelia said via telepathy.

Taranee's voice answered from a few feet beyond the huffing, puffing Laurent.

"Oh, I can do better than that," she quipped, "without even using my powers."

"Whaaaaa!" Laurent cried. His feet had suddenly been swept out from under him! He landed flat on his face, squealing in surprise.

"Nice one, Taranee!" Hay Lin's voice chirped from up above. Clearly, she was flying near the treetops. "The old tripperoo works every time!"

Uriah skidded to a halt and looked back at his fallen flunky.

"Get up, you dimwit!" he bellowed. "We have to find Martin."

"*Urngh,*" Laurent groaned, struggling to get to his feet.

"Oh, poor Laurent," Will heard Taranee say. "He got all dirty."

"I'll take care of that," Irma piped up. "What he could use now is a nice, cold shower!"

Will covered her mouth with her hand to keep from laughing out loud as she watched a gush of water swirl out of the air (or rather, out of Irma's invisible palm) and douse Laurent's blond buzz cut!

"Yow!" the dude shouted, shivering as he shook the icy water out of his eyes.

Now it was Hay Lin's turn.

"To dry Laurent off quickly," she suggested from the sky, "how 'bout a nice, cold wind? Siberian, I'd say!"

Whoooosh!

Laurent staggered backward as a gust of air—powered by Hay Lin's magic—hit him in the stomach.

"What's going on?" he cried.

Finally, Will put in her own two cents' worth. "Those guys have had enough," she told her friends. "It's Uriah's turn, now."

"Hey!" Cornelia said. "We lost track of him. He was here a minute ago."

Will looked around in surprise. Cornelia was right. The big bully had disappeared!

"Whichever way Martin went," Irma noted, "that's where we'll find Uriah!"

"That way!" Will cried, pointing through the trees.

"What way?" Hay Lin quipped back. "We

can't see you pointing, remember?"

"Whoops!" Will laughed. "Well, follow the sound of my footsteps, then."

Will dashed off in pursuit of the redheaded thug. Her friends followed. They hadn't gotten far, however, before Will skidded to a halt. She'd seen something up ahead.

Martin! she thought.

About a hundred feet away, Martin, indeed, was cowering behind the thick trunk of an elm tree. He was clutching his backpack to his chest and panting in relief. "I lost them!" he sighed happily.

"Guess again, Four-eyes!" came a sinister voice.

"Oh, no!" Martin cried, peeking around the tree.

Uriah was there waiting. "I don't know what happened to Kurt and Laurent, but it doesn't matter," he growled. "I can take care of you all by myself."

Faster than even the Guardians could react, Uriah barreled into Martin, pushing him hard in the chest.

"Ooof!" Martin cried, tumbling onto his back. His backpack crashed to the ground next to him with a loud thud.

"Kurt and Laurent are going to have to miss the show," Uriah said as he pulled back his fist to punch Martin.

There's no time to run to Martin's rescue! Will thought in anguish. He's gonna get pounded! I can't watch.

Will squeezed her eyes shut and cringed. She couldn't believe the Guardians had failed Martin!

TEN

Taranee covered her mouth to keep from crying out. Uriah's fist was just inches away from Martin's nose!

If only I could use my power on that rotten coward, she fumed. But a flying fireball would be pretty extreme, even for the likes of Uriah. Which means, I'm helpless. Martin's gonna get majorly hurt!

"I'll tell Kurt and Laurent all about this!" Uriah was saying to his quaking prey as he reared back for his punch.

"Then, tell them about this part, too!"

Taranee and her friends gasped as a new figure suddenly entered the fray. Leaping out from behind a tree, a shaggy-haired boy in a green jacket grabbed Uriah's fist, just before it connected with Martin's face.

"Huh?" Uriah gasped. He struggled to a get a glance at the intruder looming behind him.

"That's enough, Uriah!" the guy growled.

The bully finally looked over his shoulder to get a glimpse of the intruder.

"You!" he yelled.

And by "you," he meant . . .

"Nigel!" Taranee exclaimed. "That's Nigel!"

For the moment, she was glad to be invisible. She could tell that on her face was plastered a gushy, gooey, love-struck smile. She probably looked ridiculous. And Irma, for one, wouldn't have hesitated to point that out!

Not that Taranee cared. Now that she knew that Nigel hadn't reverted to his delinquent ways, she felt incredibly happy. Irma's jokes would bounce off her like soap bubbles.

Uriah was less thrilled about Nigel's freedom. His reaction, in fact, was downright violent. Shaking his arm out of Nigel's grip, he sprang to his feet. "You showed up just in time, old pal," he snarled. "There was something I wanted to tell you!"

In one deft motion, Uriah snatched Martin's backpack off the ground, while Martin himself scuttled out of the way. Then the bully swung the blue bag—weighty with books—at Nigel. Nigel staggered backward to avoid being clobbered.

Good save! Taranee thought.

Uriah swung the bag again. This time, it caught Nigel right in the chest.

Oh, no, I spoke too soon, Taranee thought. She winced as Nigel grunted and fell down on the grass, struggling to catch his breath.

That gave Uriah ample time to lift the heavy book bag over his head. "You forgot about your friends, Nigel," he said, "but they haven't forgotten about you!"

No! Taranee thought. Her legs had been frozen in place, but the idea of ten pounds of books hurtling toward Nigel's totally cute face finally unfroze them.

No way, she thought, am I going to let that happen.

She was just whipping up some fiery ammo to shoot the backpack out of Uriah's hands when she was surprised by an interruption.

And she wasn't the only one.

Tap, tap, tap.

"Excuse me!"

Someone was tapping on Uriah's shoulder. Startled, Uriah glanced behind him. That was the only opportunity the intruder needed.

Baaam!

The intruder punched Uriah so hard the big bully was practically knocked out.

"Nobody treats my backpack like that!" the boy declared.

"Nice shot, Martin!" Nigel cried, jumping to his feet in relief as Uriah slumped to the ground.

Irma hooted in disbelief. Cornelia gasped. Hay Lin cheered. But Taranee could only clasp her hands with joy as Nigel slung an arm around the bespectacled geek-turned-hero.

"Sorry I didn't get here sooner," he said. "I started following you the minute you left school, but then I lost track of you."

"Don't apologize," Martin laughed, taking off his glasses to give them a polishing. "You saved my frames, friend!"

As Uriah sat on the grass, shaking his head woozily, Martin and Nigel ambled out of the park. To judge by his wild hand gestures, Martin was recounting every detail of the ordeal for Nigel, who simply smiled, nodded, and listened to Martin's story patiently.

He's gonna be listening for a long time! Taranee thought with a giddy smile. "Ohhhh," she sighed. "Nigel is such a great guy."

Now she wished she weren't invisible. She longed to run after Nigel and grab his hand, shower him with praise for his rescue, and apologize for ever doubting him.

For Will, though, romance was pretty low on the priority list.

"So, that's over and done with!" she announced. "Now we can finally get down to business."

Taranee sighed again, but this time with regret.

So soon? she thought. I guess there's no rest for the world-saving weary.

"Since there's nothing left for us to do here," Will went on, "we should leave for Meridian right away."

"By now," Irma added, "the astral drops we made earlier will have gotten back home."

Taranee pictured her own astral drop, the magical double she'd made of herself before setting out for this mission. Her astral drop was a perfect copy, right down to her beaded braids and bookish ways. Taranee's astral drop would probably have been settled on her bed right then, reading a book, just the way Taranee herself usually did after school.

Taranee pictured Hay Lin's astral drop painting a whimsical picture, and Will's slumped in front of the TV. Irma's, true to form, would have been chowing down on an after-school snack with her mom and her little brother.

Taranee shivered. She hated the whole astral drop idea, even though it was completely necessary. The doubles always gave her the creeps.

Then again, why should the astral drops be different from any other part of this mission, she thought, as the girls quickly made their way down the street and hopped on a bus headed for the fairgrounds. I mean, what's more creepy than an old abandoned carnival?

When the Guardians arrived at the amusement park a little later, Taranee got her answer—hardly anything! She cringed as she and her friends began to pick their way through the litter-strewn carnival grounds.

"Watch your step!" Irma warned, pointing up at a rickety roller coaster track that looked as though it were about to collapse. "This place is falling apart!"

"It must have been beautiful once," Cornelia sighed. "When my dad was little, he used to come here every Sunday."

Somberly, the girls kept walking. They'd just rounded a corner when Will suddenly groaned, clutched her head, and staggered slightly.

"Hang on," she moaned. "I feel something!"

"We're there, then! Will's sixth sense is back in action," Hay Lin announced.

Whenever Will was close to a surge of Metamoorian magic, she began to experience dizziness, clammy skin, the whole nine yards.

That must feel awful, Taranee thought, grabbing Will's arms to prevent her from slumping to the muddy ground. Leadership sure comes at a cost!

It took Will only a few minutes to overcome her queasiness. Once she was back on her feet, she looked around. "Aha," she said.

She pointed at a river of murky water, complete with a couple of boats shaped like swans. The stream led into a heart-shaped "Tunnel of Love."

"The portal must be in there," Will said.

Taranee looked at the creepy ride. If it had been a different time, Taranee would have loved to go on the ride with Nigel. But just then the ride wasn't looking so appealing.

Irma seemed to be feeling the same dread. She wrinkled up her nose as she looked over at the deserted ride. "Are you really sure that's it?" she asked Will. "Before crawling into that *hole*, it'd be nice to have a little more assurance!"

Cornelia snorted, then hopped into the man-made river. Knee-deep in the slimy water, she turned back to Irma. "Move it or lose it, Irma," she ordered. "Will has never been wrong before!"

Wow, Taranee thought as she, too, stepped gingerly into the water. Cornelia used to argue with Will's every decision. Now she's her biggest defender. That's almost more unbeliev-able than the fact that we're all Guardians!

Taranee would have giggled at the thought—if she hadn't been so scared. *And* if her feet hadn't been so uncomfortably soggy.

From the looks on their faces, Will, Cornelia, and Hay Lin were just as grossed out as Taranee by stepping through the murk. Their disgust was *not* lost on Irma.

"So Will hasn't been wrong before," she protested from dry land. "But there's a first time for everything. Can't I take one of those swan boats? This swamp does *not* look very inviting to me."

"You're the one who controls water," Cornelia snapped. "If you don't want to get your feet wet, why don't you use your powers?"

Will sloshed in the water as she spun around, cutting the girls off. "That's what we're all about to do," she said. "Get ready to transform, gals. It's time to use the Heart of Candracar!"

Will thrust her right fist out and threw her head back. Soon, jets of pink magic escaped from between her fingers and began to swirl around her.

Here we go, Taranee thought. As the cyclone of magic moved around Will, a mix of emotions whirled inside Taranee. She was scared, sure, but she was also feeling something much bigger than fear. She was brimming with eager confidence. She was ready to take on Phobos!

First though, Taranee had to be zapped by the Heart of Candracar. The magical amulet would transform her into her Guardian shape: with a taller, curvier, stronger body; with hair that bounced around her head in shiny tendrils; with a supercool, midriff-baring top, snug purple shorts, funky, striped leggings, and wings.

I'll look different, Taranee thought, as the magic hit her with a jolt. But I'll still be me—a Guardian of the Veil who's ready for anything!

ELEVEN

Will took a deep breath, then slowly opened her eyes and looked down at herself. Yup, it was all there: body-skimming purple and turquoise clothes; long, muscular arms and legs; and, of course, purple boots.

Once again, the Heart of Candracar had transformed her and her friends into superpowerful Guardians.

Now we just to have to hope, Will thought, that this Tunnel of Love actually leads us to a portal.

Motioning to her friends, Will plunged into the heart-shaped passageway. As the light from the outside world waned, the tunnel— with its cracked wooden walls and faded paintings of hearts and cherubs—grew creepier and creepier. Will couldn't help wondering if there were fish, or worse, swimming around in that cloudy river.

Keep it together, Will told herself. One screech at some imagined eel and Irma's gonna lose it. She's already complaining.

"Man!" Irma said, right on cue. "Now my boots are filling up with mud."

"Oh, please," Cornelia sniped, glancing over her shoulder at Irma. "I feel like I'm on a secret mission with my grandma! Will you give it a rest?"

"Cut it out, you two," Hay Lin said suddenly. "Take a look at that!"

Will had been so intent on feeling her way through the dark water that she hadn't even glanced toward the end of the tunnel. Now she looked up to see what Hay Lin was so excited about.

Up ahead was a round, silvery hoop that seemed to be floating in the darkness. The hoop roiled about, spitting sparks of hot magic. It couldn't have looked more unwelcoming.

Still, Will was happy to see it!

"It's the portal we've been looking for!" she cried. "Vathek came through here."

Together, the girls began to run toward the portal.

Will couldn't help feeling a pang of terror as she led the way. The Guardians had already crossed through the Veil to Metamoor several times. Each crossing had been more treacherous than the last. Once, Cornelia had landed in the bottom of a fountain and almost drowned. Another journey had shrunk the Guardians to the size of peas and landed them in an aquarium with a flesh-eating fish.

I wonder what horrible trial is going to hit us now, Will thought. Not that I can turn back or anything.

Holding her breath, she dived through the ring of silver magic.

In a series of sizzly whooshes, her friends followed her.

To Will's surprise, they emerged directly into a cobblestoned street! The moment the fifth Guardian—Irma, of course—stepped through the portal, it disappeared into the shadows beneath a stone stairwell.

"Wow!" Cornelia exclaimed.

"That was too easy!" Taranee said. "So easy that I'm wondering if we're in the right place. If this is Meridian, it sure has changed."

"Do you we think we took a wrong turn?" Irma asked.

Will was curious, too. The last time the Guardians had been in the vast Metamoorian city, the people's attitudes had been as gray as the sky. They'd tromped through the dirty streets, their heads down, with scowls on their faces. Will had felt Phobos's evil rule everywhere.

Today there was no evidence of any such despair. The streets were teeming with happy people—well, happy Metamoorians, anyway. These citizens of Metamoor looked like pointy-eared green lizards, or lumpish, cobalt-colored monsters. In spite of their leathery skin, red eyes, and clawed hands, though, Metamoorians were just like human beings. They yearned for happiness. For freedom. For someone to give them hope.

They yearned for someone like the Light of Meridian, Will realized, wide-eyed. Elyon! "This must be a celebration of the coronation ceremony," she said to her friends. "We got here just in time!"

"Then we don't have a moment to lose,"

Cornelia said. "We have to find Elyon and stay by her side."

"Which means we have to find a way in to Phobos's castle!" Hay Lin added from the rear of the group.

Will frowned. Her shoulders slumped. *Another* obstacle! Would they never . . .

Hey, wait a minute! Will realized suddenly. This problem is actually *totally* solvable. I can't believe I forgot!

She didn't have time to explain her solution to her friends. She merely looked around to gauge the girls' locations, then turned on her heel and began running. "Follow me!" she called to her fellow Guardians. "I know a short-cut."

Without a word, the girls went after her. The Guardians' great strength carried them to Will in no time. They skidded to a halt several feet shy of a thicket of roses with petals as black and lush as velvet.

Naturally, Irma stretched a curious finger toward one of the beautiful, dark blossoms.

Will jumped out to intercept Irma before she touched the bloom. "On the other side of this thicket is the palace garden," Will explained. "But these roses are enchanted. They're poisoned! I had a nasty run-in with them once before. Remember when my dormouse dashed into a portal and I had to chase him all over Meridian? Luckily, the poison only makes Guardians fall asleep."

"But," Will said, looking at Cornelia, "these flowers are no match for Cornelia."

"I sure hope you're right," Cornelia replied with a grimace. Shaking a few strands of her silky blond hair out of her eyes, she held her hands out before her. They began to glow with green magic and vibrate with earth power. Finally, a stream of energy erupted from her palms with a loud *zaaaamm!*

Cornelia's magic carved a narrow but passable trail through the rose garden. Cornelia squinted and grimaced with the effort of holding the roses aside.

"And," Irma said as Cornelia worked her magic, "once we're inside Phobos's garden, *then* what do we do?"

"Just what we always do," Will replied. "Make it up as we go along!"

Yeah, she thought with a gulp. I just hope our usual method doesn't blow up in our faces.

"Come on!" Cornelia cried from near the roses. "Hurry up! The magic in these flowers is really strong, and I don't know how much longer I'll be able to keep the passageway open."

Gasping in alarm, Will sprinted through the opening. The trio at her heels tumbled after her. They all looked back, scared, at Cornelia. Her arms were shaking, and her face was bright red. Pretty soon, she'd have to break her hold on the roses. Finally, she let go and started to run.

As she dashed toward her friends, the poisonous branches started to close in after her. As she neared the end of the trail, Cornelia took a flying leap. She made it—barely! She skidded in the dirt just beyond the rose thicket, disheveled but unharmed.

"Nice work, Corny!" Irma said with no trace of sarcasm.

Will was helping her heroic friend to her feet when a voice rang out behind her. It was a gentle, familiar voice.

"Well, well, this is certainly a surprise!"

Will spun around, then grinned happily at the visitor. "Hey!" she cried. "I was really hoping to see you, Daltar!"

Will rushed over to shake her friend's callused hand and smile up into his face—pleasantly colored with green slashes and adorned with a superhero-style red mask. Meanwhile, her friends huddled together and whispered. Will overheard Hay Lin say: "That must be the gardener she told us about."

Hay Lin was right. Will had met Daltar when she'd awakened from the woozy, black-rose-induced nap she had had after chasing her dormouse into the garden. Daltar had told Will his story, and they had become allies.

Like so many in Meridian, Daltar's life had been ruined by Phobos. The evil prince had forced the humble gardener to create the sinister barrier of blooms around his garden. And to make sure that Daltar would never leave the delicate flowers untended, Phobos had turned the man's wife and daughter themselves into black roses. Living as blooms, the mother and daughter were now lost in the vast thicket. So Daltar preserved each flower with the utmost care, yearning for a way to break the curse and be reunited with his family.

Restoring the Light of Meridian was a good way to start, Will thought. She was eager to tell

Daltar her plan and hear his opinion.

"It's nice to see you again, young lady," the gardener said with a sweet but sad smile. "And your friends must be—"

"You got it!" Will said, interrupting him. "These are the four other Guardians of the Veil. We've come back to protect Elyon."

"She may be facing grave danger!" Cornelia said.

"The danger you speak of is named Phobos," Daltar said. "The prince is plotting something. For some time now, he's been secluding himself in his underground hide-away, the Abyss of Shadows. That's *not* a good sign."

"From the name," Irma added, "I'd guess it's not a very cheery place, either."

Daltar nodded. Will grabbed his shoulders. In her Guardian form she was almost as tall as he was.

"We have to talk to Elyon right away," she insisted.

"That won't be easy," Daltar said, running a hand through his hair. "The princess is in her chambers, and Murmurers are roaming through the castle. But I might be able to help you."

Will smiled at Daltar gleefully.

I never expected to make true friends in Metamoor, she thought, let alone friends who might help us save the world. Somehow, I think I'm becoming accustomed to this strange land, just as I am adjusting to Heatherfield.

Let's just hope, she thought with a bit more trepidation, that Daltar's plan works and I get to see my city again!

TWELVE

Gazing into her ten-foot-tall, gilded mirror, Elyon almost didn't recognize herself.

Who is that girl in the flowing purple gown and gossamer wrap? she thought as she twisted back and forth shyly. That girl couldn't be plain little Elyon Brown, could it? This Elyon is elegant, gorgeous, regal!

At least, Elyon thought with a happy giggle, that's what everyone from the Sheffield Institute would say if they could see me now.

However, she said, scolding herself, this is no time to think about people from the past. I'll be Metamoor's queen soon. I need to make new friends here—people who can help me make this place into a healthier, happier world. It's going to take some major work.

But today, I'm just going to enjoy myself. I think, as Light of Meridian, I'm entitled to at least one day of happiness! And I can start right after Master Jink is done with these tedious alterations!

Elyon looked down from the pedestal on which she was standing. Master Jink, a wizened old tailor, was making tiny stitches in the hem of her dress. "You're stunning," the little creature exclaimed, shoving the sleeves of his plain, gray robe farther up his skinny arms. "One more stitch or two, and we'll be done."

"I really hope so, Master Jink," Elyon said with a generous smile.

The creature was pulling a last length of purple thread through the hem of Elyon's gown when someone knocked at the grand, glass doors of the chamber.

"Huh?" Master Jink squawked. "I asked that we not be disturbed. Who could that be?"

"I don't know," Elyon said. With a mischievous look at the agitated little tailor, she added, "Let's find out! Come in."

The doors swung open to reveal a man with green slashes on his cheeks and a red mask over his eyes. Cedric had a mask like that, but his was menacing. This man, it seemed to Elyon, covered his eyes not to intimidate anyone, but to hide. Everything about his stature—from his sagging shoulders to his slackened jaw to the dullness of his blue-gray ponytail—spelled grief.

Everything, that is, except for the gorgeous bouquet in the man's hands. Elyon found it hard to believe that such vibrantly colored flowers could flourish in gray old Metamoor. They must have come from Phobos's garden—the only spot in Meridian where greenery thrived.

That meant that this man was an ally. Or was he?

"Please forgive my intrusion, Your Radiant Highness," the man said softly, bowing. "I bring you our most beautiful flowers to adorn your hair."

Flowers? Elyon thought. Flowers? Master Jink and I specifically discussed *ribbons*. Lots of shimmery, purple ribbons. No flowers!

"There must be some mistake," Elyon replied, confused. "I didn't ask for anything of the sort."

"With," the man added, bowing even more

deeply, "the best wishes of Will and your other friends, who are waiting for you in the garden."

Elyon gasped softly. A moment later, she dropped her gaze to the floor, in shame. Just the mention of her friends brought her back to the present.

Elyon had a hunch that, if her friends had come all the way from Heatherfield on that particular day, something was wrong.

Without another word, she stepped off her pedestal and hurried from her bedchamber, the gardener silent at her side.

"But, Your Highness," Master Jink called after her in confusion.

Elyon didn't have time to explain herself to the sweet old creature. Nor did she know what she would even have said. So, she simply hurried away without another word.

She followed the gardener down, down, down, through the palace's convoluted corridors, then out into Phobos's garden. Elyon gasped. She'd seen the garden before, but its beauty had not ceased to amaze her, especially after she had spent so much time gazing out over the rest of Meridian's gray landscape.

Daltar put a finger to his lips and led Elyon

through more tunnels and corridors filled with trellises, topiaries, and trees that formed gentle arches over grassy paths.

Finally, the pair stopped in a tiny, shady grove deep within the garden. Waiting there—looking almost as exotic as the gorgeous blooms that surrounded them—were the Guardians of the Veil. Elyon's friends.

"You! You've come back for me!" Elyon exclaimed.

"Yes, Elyon!" Will said, stepping forward. Her face was tense and urgent. "We don't have much time, so listen to what we have to tell you. Then, you'll have to make up your mind about what you want to do!"

THIRTEEN

As Cedric stood in his own small bedchamber, preparing for the coronation, he was amazed at how calm he felt. He supposed that a self-righteous little human—say, *Elyon*—would have used a different word for his demeanor. She'd have called him smug.

All right, *smug*, Cedric thought with an evil laugh. I have every reason to be. Phobos is just minutes away from seizing Elyon's power— power he should have had years ago, power that he will then share with me! And when Meridian's citizens rise up in anger, after their precious princess has been destroyed, Phobos's Annihilators will keep us safe.

The plan, Cedric thought with great satisfaction, was foolproof.

Now, all I have to do, he thought, is remain calm when I reach Phobos's chamber. The prince cannot be allowed to think that I claim any part of this victory. The day's glory will belong only to him.

Cedric smoothed back his long, blond hair and made his face expressionless. He left his room and began the short trek to Phobos's royal suite. When he arrived, the prince was pacing the marble floor, wearing his finest turquoise robe. He radiated victory.

"The procession is ready, sire," Cedric informed his master, bowing.

"Excellent!" Phobos declared. "Call for my sister. She will walk by my side."

"I'm already here, Phobos."

Cedric lifted one eyebrow and wheeled, his flowing robe swirling around him. This was not part of his plan. He had meant to fetch Elyon from her bedchamber, then keep close tabs on her every move during those last—but crucial—moments of her life as princess of Metamoor.

Cedric gave Elyon a long, hard look. He searched for the impudent expression she'd been wearing during the past few days. It wasn't there. Elyon looked placid and pale, even a little dazed.

Perhaps she's finally realized the gravity of her position as future queen, Cedric thought, suppressing a laugh. Little does she know.

"Elyon!" Phobos called, jolting Cedric out of his reverie. The prince bounded over to his sister. His smile, if possible, was even wider than before.

"Are you excited?" he asked her. "The long-awaited moment has finally arrived, and the crown will soon be yours!"

Cedric strode over to the open chest in the center of the chamber and lifted a red, silken pillow from inside. Nestled on the cushion and glowing with magical energy was Elyon's bejeweled crown.

"Yes," Elyon said in a dreamy voice. "I'm excited. I just hope I'm worthy, my brother."

Cedric bowed his head so Elyon could not see the smile once again tugging at his lips.

Oh, don't worry, my little Elyon, he thought. You'll do *just* fine.

Within a few minutes, the procession had begun. Flanked by dozens of soldiers, Phobos and Elyon walked through a crowd of Metamoorians. Cedric followed them, still holding the crown.

The citizens' cheers filled Cedric's head like a pounding drumbeat. He was stunned by the size of the crowd. Thousands had turned out to cheer their new ruler.

Thousands upon thousands, Cedric corrected himself nervously. He glanced over his shoulder. The phalanx of soldiers behind him was at least ten rows deep.

They'll keep us safe, Cedric thought with a shaky intake of breath—I hope.

Returning his attention to the procession, he tried to close his ears to the grating sound of the peasants' cheers. Still, a few of their shouts made it through.

"Long live Elyon!" cried a little boy with green ears.

"Long live the princess," shouted a cloaked woman with blue claws.

"Long live the Light of Meridian!" yelled another Metamoorian.

Cedric shook his head. Silly fools, he thought. As if they knew what was good for them.

Over the heads of the crowd, Cedric spotted a raised platform, capped by an elegant canopy of red silk. Soldiers had already encircled the stage and were keeping the crowd at bay.

Good, Cedric thought. We're almost there. The plan is working.

"Hey!" chirped a voice from somewhere to his left. "These folks seem really happy!"

That voice, Cedric thought, cocking his head. It sounds familiar.

Cedric moved his gaze from his master and Elyon—for just a moment—to scan the people nearby. He saw six slim creatures, draped in the ugly brown cloaks of Metamoor's lowliest peasants. Their faces were hidden by their hoods.

They're probably too ugly to look upon, Cedric sniffed disdainfully. They're completely inconsequential.

He continued slowly behind Phobos and Elyon toward the stage, trying in vain to ignore the other snatches of conversation that wafted out of the crowd.

"Huh!" said a gurgly voice. "Why shouldn't we be happy? That usurper, Phobos, has finally understood that it's time for him to step down. Look at that arrogant smile on his face. And to think that until today he's never lowered himself to walk among us."

"Yah!" said another throaty creature. "The princess should punish him for all the wrong he's done us."

Cedric clenched his sharp jaw as he listened to the citizens berate Phobos. Normally, such traitorous statements would have been grounds for instant punishment. And Cedric would have been happy to do the punishing.

Today however, Cedric thought with grim satisfaction, these creatures are not to be trifled with. A punishment worse than prison awaits them soon enough.

"See who's here?"

Cedric cocked his head. This latest voice also sounded familiar, not to mention reedy, feminine, and decidedly flirty!

"It's Vathek and Caleb!" the voice continued. "I bet this place is full of rebels ready to make their move if something goes wrong."

"It seems we're not the only ones who are worried," said a third female voice.

Meaningless, these statements, Cedric reminded himself, as the royal procession finally reached the stage. No amount of rebels can overpower our army. We'll be fine, fine, fine.

"Look!" piped up a squeaky voice somewhere near Cedric, in the center of the round platform. "The ceremony's starting!"

Cedric held his breath as Phobos positioned himself at the front of the platform. At his side was Elyon, looking small and delicate.

"People of Meridian," Phobos said. His voice, amplified by unseen magic, boomed out over the audience. "Today is a joyful day for our city and for the entire kingdom of Metamoor."

Phobos turned to Elyon, whose eyes were wide and glistening. "A kingdom," he added, "that for too long has been deprived of its legitimate queen and instead ruled by a brother who, for too long, was deprived of his beloved sister."

Cedric bowed his head and closed his eyes. His master's devious prose was awe-inspiring. Cedric wanted to savor every second of that moment—

"At least he's being honest!" a voice in the crowd said.

Cedric's eyes opened with a snap. It was that impudent, flirty voice, chirping annoyingly again!

"I mean," she continued, "he's right about being wrong!"

"Shhh!" replied the girl's companion.

Even though Cedric wanted permanently to silence the crowd, he simply returned his attention to Phobos and Elyon. Phobos was signaling to him to bring the crown. Cedric stepped forward and held the cushion toward his master, his hands trembling with emotion.

"And so," Phobos said, lifting the glowing crown from the pillow, "I bestow upon you, Elyon, this symbol of justice and wisdom, of honor and loyalty. May your eternal power illuminate the spirit and the path of your loyal subjects."

Cedric held his breath as Phobos began to fit the magical crown over Elyon's shaggy blond hair. The girl's head was bowed, her eyes closed.

"No longer," Phobos proclaimed, "to be called *princess* of Meridian."

There! Cedric saw Elyon's shoulders hunch with pain. Her chest began heaving. She was gasping for breath and stumbling blindly.

"And no longer to be among us!" Phobos added with a maniacal cackle.

"*Aaaayyeeeeeee!*"

Elyon's scream pierced the gray air like a hot, white light. It was a shriek of desperate pain and suffering.

"Wh—what's happening?" a creature cried from the crowd.

"It was a trap!" another bellowed.

Cedric held his breath as he watched Elyon's body go slack. She fell to the stage with a heavy thud.

"I'm sorry, my dear, sweet Elyon," Phobos cackled, "but in the end, it's better this way. You were so young. You would have ended up wasting your immense power, while I know how to use it."

Phobos bent over his fallen sister. He cradled her head in his hands, his eyes cold and unfeeling. The girl's head lolled loosely.

Elyon was dead.

Laughing once again, Phobos snatched the crown from her head. He gazed at the pulsing, glowing object in delight.

"Phobos is a monster!" a woman screamed

from somewhere in the crowd.

"Villain!" agreed another.

"Criminal!"

"Traitor. *Traitor!*"

Cedric stepped over Elyon's body, kicking the hem of her long purple skirt out of his way. He sidled up behind the prince. "Sire," he warned, "the crowd is furious."

"Oh, don't worry. Let them yell, Cedric," Phobos said, gesturing at the masses.

The rebellion was already starting. The usually humble creatures of Metamoor were beginning to surge toward the stage, eager to rip the prince to shreds. They were not making much headway: with little effort and much menace, Phobos's soldiers clubbed the rabble, driving them back.

"These miserable peasants," Phobos said over the roar of the crowd, "will be the first to taste my new power. Elyon's energy still lies within this crown, but in a moment, it will have a new master!"

Reverentially, Phobos placed the crown upon his own gleaming, blond head.

Cedric held his breath.

Phobos stood stock-still.

"How—how do you feel?" Cedric asked cautiously.

"I'm not sure," Phobos said, glancing up toward the light that was still pulsing from the crown. "There's only one way to find out whether the spell has worked. I will—" Phobos turned toward the crowd and thrust his arm out toward them. "—I will do away with these worthless creatures with a wave of my hand!" he yelled wildly. His arm trembled with magic and exultation.

Cedric gasped with pleasure. This was the moment he'd been waiting for all his life. His master was about to ascend to the highest plane of power.

"Detestable people of Meridian," Phobos raved. "I have always longed to do this. Ha-ha! Ha-ha-ha—uh, ha?"

"Huh?" Cedric gasped, in horrible disappointment. Phobos's wrathful blast of magic, the one that was supposed to wipe out Meridian's entire population in one fell swoop, had done nothing.

The citizens remained thronged in front of him, their faces more stunned and angry than ever.

One of them in particular was moving swiftly through the crowd. She kept her head lowered and hidden beneath the hood of her brown cloak until she reached Phobos's feet. Then, she pulled the hood back to reveal a shock of glossy red hair and a pair of large, brown eyes.

It's Will! Cedric thought.

"Don't strain yourself, Phobos," Will said. "Your new powers don't exist!"

Normally, Cedric would have laughed off such an arrogant statement and watched his master destroy the girl. But there was nothing normal about this moment—or this messenger. Cedric realized that she was herself brimming with power.

She's the Keeper of the Heart of Candracar! Cedric thought in terror. What have the Guardians of the Veil done to Phobos's plan?

FOURTEEN

Cornelia eagerly peeked out from beneath the hood of her brown cloak. She couldn't wait to hear Phobos's reaction to what Will was about to tell him.

Will had already made an impact when she pulled her hood back to reveal her identity. Cornelia saw Cedric go pale with terror when he recognized the Keeper of the Heart.

Now Will moved closer to her foe. She stopped only when she reached the edge of the stage. Still hidden beneath their hoods, Cornelia and the other Guardians crowded close behind her.

"Your new powers don't exist," Will said to the mad tyrant, "because what you absorbed on the stage wasn't the real

Elyon. It was only a living replica that we created!"

"The Guardians!" Cedric gasped, as if he'd been trying to say the word for many seconds but had only now found the breath to do so.

Phobos, of course, was more concerned with the body lying at his feet, the young girl in the purple gown.

"The . . . the real Elyon?" he stuttered. His eyes grew wide with confusion. For the first time since he'd stepped into the city square, his smirk melted away. "What does all of this mean?"

Cornelia felt a rustling next to her. She peeked out of her cloak just in time to see another brown hood being thrown backward. From it emerged an elfin face capped by shaggy, straw-colored bangs.

"It means, dear brother, that I'm right here."

That's my cue, Cornelia thought. She threw off her own heavy hood. Nearby, Taranee, Hay Lin, and Irma revealed themselves as well. But Cornelia had eyes only for her best friend. She was proud of Elyon, standing up to her sinister brother like that.

"It's the princess!" Cedric shrieked.

"I've been tricked!" Phobos bellowed in anger, clenching his fists and gaping at the lifeless, vanishing image of Elyon at his feet.

Who's the conqueror of the universe *now?* Cornelia thought with amusement.

Behind her, a male voice called out.

"The day of reckoning has arrived, Phobos!"

At the sound of the voice—deep, yet clear as a bell—Cornelia's heart began to pound and her hands began to shake. And then, a huge smile spread across her face.

"Caleb!" Cornelia called.

Over the heads of peasants battling soldiers, of big, blue Vathek, pummeling every enemy who crossed his path, over the chaos of battle, Cornelia spotted her love. How could she have missed him? Even in soldier mode, Caleb looked sweet and kind, from his shiny brown hair to his green-striped cheeks to his liquid brown eyes.

Holding his sword above his head, Caleb elbowed his way through the crowd. It seemed to take forever for him to reach Cornelia. When he finally made it, the pair stared into each other's stunned eyes for what seemed like another hour, neither one saying a word.

In truth, it all lasted only a few seconds. But that was enough time for Cornelia to say a thousand things to the boy—in her heart, at least.

She wondered what would happen if they defeated Phobos. Perhaps they could finally be together.

She continued staring at him as she reminisced about seeing Caleb the first time. He'd been only an image that Cornelia had conjured in a daydream. Yet even then, she'd loved him. When she'd found him in Metamoor, she had realized he was her destiny.

Cornelia said all of those things the only way she could in such circumstances—with her eyes.

The moment was sublime. It also, of course, had to end. There was a battle to fight—a fact that Caleb clearly regretted. His voice shook as he spoke the next words.

"Cornelia," he breathed, "I'm so happy you're here."

Cornelia opened her mouth to reply, but Vathek, bellowing nearby, cut her off. "Everyone!" he ordered. "Get Phobos and

Cedric. This is our chance!"

Caleb glanced at Vathek, then turned back to Cornelia. His eyes had regained their fire. He was ready to fight.

So little time, Cornelia thought, a lump forming in her throat.

"Be safe," Caleb said, gazing deeply into Cornelia's eyes. Then, with a rakish grin, he slipped into the crowd.

For a moment, Cornelia was so blissfully devastated she couldn't move. Unfortunately, the shrill, cowardly voice of Cedric, who was still cowering on the nearby stage, destroyed her reverie.

"It's a rebellion, Your Highness!" he cried.

"I'll destroy them!" Phobos answered in a malevolent growl. "I'll do away with them all. Every last one of them! Arise, Annihilators! *Rise up and destroy those who dared disobey the master of Meridian.*"

BROOOOOOMMMMMM.

Cornelia stumbled, crashing into Will as the ground rumbled beneath her feet. A moment later, the street cracked and crumbled—to make way for the most horrific creatures Cornelia had ever seen! They were a cross between dinosaurs and robots, with red masks and blank expressions. Everything about them, Cornelia saw, was built for battle, from their immense height to the helmets that enveloped their skulls to the tortoiseshell armor that girded their torsos.

There were hundreds of them, Cornelia quickly determined. As they finished their ascent, their eyes began to flash with ominous red sparks.

"Friends of yours, Hay Lin?" Irma said.

"Actually, by the looks of them," Hay Lin quipped back, "I thought they were *your* friends."

Ka-ZAAMMMM! Ka-ZAAAAMMMM!

There was no more time to joke. The Annihilators had begun shooting red bolts of lightning from their eyes! Bedlam broke out as the poor Metamoorians scrambled to escape the beams.

Well, that confirms it, Cornelia thought. Those guys are no friends to any of us!

Reluctantly, Cornelia stopped thinking about Caleb. She didn't have time to swoon. She had an evil prince to hunt!

I also have to rescue Elyon, Cornelia

realized. Her eyes widened as she saw Phobos point at her friend.

"Accursed Elyon!" Phobos yelled. "Get her, Cedric! Don't let her escape."

Vathek heard that, too, even as he was clobbering four soldiers at once elsewhere. With one thug in a headlock and another on his back, Vathek spun around to yell at Cornelia and her friends.

"Take the princess to safety!" he cried.

Good idea, Cornelia thought. She turned to Elyon, who was already being swept away by a woman with bright pink hair and slick, chartreuse skin. Cornelia thought the woman must have been a Murmurer who'd defied her master.

Cedric leaped off the stage and shoved Cornelia aside to get at Elyon. Grabbing her skinny arm, he grunted, "You're not going anywhere, little girl!"

Elyon scowled. Then she flung out her arm and hit Cedric in the chest with a blast of white magic. He went flying, landing on his back ten feet away.

"Ugh!" he grunted.

"I've had enough of you, Cedric," Elyon spat, her eyes blazing.

With Cedric now dazed, Elyon grabbed the Murmurer's hand. The princess and the creature both covered their heads with their brown hoods and melted into the crowd. Within seconds, they'd slipped away from the skirmish.

Cornelia sighed. Her friend was safe. That, she thought wearily, only leaves, oh, about a million other folks to save.

Out of the corner of her eye, Cornelia espied a soldier bearing down upon her, waving his sword.

Cornelia threw out her hand. A stream of green magic shot from her palm, connecting with the sword and shattering it like a piece of crystal. "Ha!" Cornelia cried. She looked around for another foe. As she did, she saw that Hay Lin was airborne, blasting soldiers with gusts of frigid wind, and that Taranee was hurling fireballs.

Will, however, had another enemy in mind. "Come on, girls," she called to her crew. "We can't let Phobos get away."

"No!" came a determined reply.

Cornelia gasped. That was Caleb! He'd just emerged from a tangle of wounded and whimpering soldiers. He lifted his sword and declared bravely, "The prince is mine!"

Without another word, Caleb leaped onto the stage to confront the evil prince. Cornelia felt her heart lurch with both pride and fear.

"Caleb!" Phobos snarled. "I've heard your name mentioned a great deal lately. So, it's true! You've rebelled against your master."

"You're not master of anything, Phobos," Caleb growled. "Nothing you see around you is yours."

"And to think," Phobos said sarcastically, "that you were nothing, Caleb. You were only a poor Murmurer."

Cornelia clutched her throat. So that was the explanation behind the green slashes that striped Caleb's cheeks. His flower-petal skin. His beautiful soul. He'd been a Murmurer, born in Phobos's flower garden.

"A Murmurer," Caleb confirmed. "But one capable of reason! When I opened my eyes, I understood right away what side I should be on."

With no warning, Caleb slashed at Prince Phobos with his sword. The blade *whooshed* through the air impressively, but Phobos deflected it with a magical flick of his wrist.

Cornelia held her breath.

"A Murmurer with a will of its own is a mistake," Phobos spat, "and there's only one thing to do with mistakes."

Fzzzaaaakkk!

"Aaagh!" Caleb cried out in pain.

Phobos had just flung a lightning bolt right into Caleb's stomach. Cornelia screamed as she watched her love double over, clutching his side.

A moment later, all she saw was Phobos.

Her target.

Her mortal enemy.

"He's attacking Caleb," Cornelia shouted to Will, who neatly shattered the staff of an ax with her forearm. "I have to help him!"

Cornelia began sprinting toward the stage. All she could think of—all she could live for at that moment—was Caleb. That must have been why she barely heard Will's shout: "Look out, Cornelia!"

Feeling as if she were moving in slow motion, Cornelia glanced back at her friend. That gave her just enough time to see an Annihilator's red lightning bolt heading right for her head! She had no time to evade it.

Caleb, Cornelia thought wanly. Elyon.

Heatherfield.

I'll never see them agai—

"Ooof!" Cornelia grunted. Will had just tackled her with all the grace of a fullback in a football game! The two Guardians tumbled to the ground while the Annihilator's ammo sizzled over their heads, then melted into a black wisp, in the end hurting nobody.

Breathing hard, Cornelia made fists in the dirt. Her element, earth, so dear to her, wasn't helping.

Caleb and I, Cornelia thought with a sob. Will we ever know anything but these crazy contradictions? These tragic sacrifices?

Must being a Guardian, she wailed inwardly, always hurt so badly?

The question almost broke Cornelia's heart. But her strength remained intact. Using every ounce of her power, Cornelia lurched back to her feet to join her fellow Guardians—her best friends—in their fight to save the city of Meridian.

COME ON, GIRLS. WE CAN'T LET PHOBOS GET AWAY!

NO! LEAVE THE PRINCE TO ME.

ZAAM

WHAM

AH, YES, CALEB. I'VE HEARD YOUR NAME MENTIONED A GREAT DEAL LATELY. SO I GUESS IT'S TRUE. YOU'VE GONE AGAINST YOUR MASTER.

YOU'RE NOT MASTER OF ANYTHING, PHOBOS, AND DEFINITELY NOT MASTER OF ME. NOTHING YOU SEE AROUND YOU IS YOURS.

AND TO THINK THAT YOU WERE ONCE A POOR MURMURER. . . .

WRONG! I WAS A MURMURER CAPABLE OF REASON. WHEN I FINALLY OPENED MY EYES I KNEW RIGHT AWAY WHAT SIDE I SHOULD BE ON.

SHASH

A MURMURER WITH A WILL OF ITS OWN IS A MISTAKE. . . . AND THERE'S ONLY ONE THING TO DO WITH MISTAKES!

AHHH!

FZZZAK

PHOBOS IS ATTACKING CALEB. I HAVE TO HELP HIM!

LOOK OUT, CORNELIA!

CRASH

!

KAM RAM

YOUR SOLDIERS WILL NEVER STOP THE REBELLION. OUR VICTORY IS AT HAND!

... BUT YOU WON'T LIVE LONG ENOUGH TO SEE IT FOR YOURSELF!

THAT MAY BE....

AAAAAGH!

YOU'VE GONE BEYOND MY CONTROL.... YOU'VE BECOME THE LEADER OF THE DESPERATE GROUP OF REBELLIOUS METAMOORIANS.... YOU BROUGHT THEM TOGETHER AND TURNED THEM INTO A THREAT AGAINST ME....

AHHHHH! S—STOP!

AND FOR THIS, I WILL PUNISH YOU, CALEB. I CREATED YOU AS A MURMURER....

NNNH...

... AND SO A MURMURER YOU SHALL BE AGAIN.... IN ITS MOST PRIMITIVE FORM!

CALEEEEEEB! NOOOOOO!!!

OH, NO . . .

HE'S . . .
HE'S . . .

. . . HE'S FREE,
CORNELIA.
HE'S FREE.

YOUR HIGHNESS! THE ENTIRE CITY OF MERIDIAN IS UP
IN ARMS. WE'LL NEED EVERY ONE OF OUR SOLDIERS
AND ALL OF THE ANNIHILATORS TO STOP THEM.

I'M RETURNING TO THE
CASTLE! CALL IN OUR
HEAVIEST FORCES. . . .

. . . AND
DESTROY
THE CITY!